Mapmaker

Also by Margaret Bolton and published by Ginninderra Press

Not Another Nun Story

Mother and Son

Tales from Port Vic

Not Forgotten

Start with a Coffee (Pocket Poets)

Prisoners of War (Pocket People)

Margaret Bolton

Mapmaker

The life and times
of Abraham Ortelius

Mapmaker: The life and times of Abraham Ortelius
ISBN 978 1 76109 118 6
Copyright © Margaret Bolton 2021
Cover images used by courtesy of Marcel and Deborah van den Broecke

First published 2021 by
GINNINDERRA PRESS
PO Box 3461 Port Adelaide 5015
www.ginninderrapress.com.au

Contents

Part One

1527–1569

Prologue

He's getting very old now, stooped and balding, and fading fast. Racked with pain and confined to his chair. He's even finding it difficult to read any more. It's not that he can't see; it's more that he can't concentrate as waves of gripping pain roll over him.

All he can do is sit in front of the open fire and reflect. At least it's warm inside, although it's snowing outside. The flames warm his hands and feet. But his mind is as alert as ever.

He still finds some small pleasure in remembering…remembering the journey, the good times and the bad times, for there were plenty of both. He has surely been blessed throughout his life, despite all the horror that recent history has thrown our way.

And while I sit with him, he likes to remember dear family, friends and associates, many of whom have already died. To dwell again on the whispered endearments of his little ones, the heady conversations with friends and foe, the haggling for a better price in business dealings and the discussions over a frothy beer about humanist ideas. He's had a full and productive life.

Then he turns to recall all the colouring and producing of maps, both old and new, and the collecting of beautiful things. He was so proud of all the accolades that came his way when he produced the very first atlas, or mapbook as he called it, twenty years before Mercator produced his.

But above all, he remembers the books and the wealth of knowledge contained in them. He has spent his whole life learning.

This is his story, the story of my brother Abraham Ortels. I agree with Socrates, who said that the unexamined life is not worth living. I want to get it all down.

1

We lived in exciting times. Not too long before Abraham's story began, about thirty-five years beforehand, explorers set forth across the immense Atlantic Ocean in their little ships and discovered a whole new world, which is exactly what they called the new lands: the New World. At least at first; later, the new continent came to be known as the Americas. From 1492 to 1503, Christopher Columbus made four voyages westwards into the unknown to reach the Spice Islands of the Far East, but discovered much of Central America and its islands. In 1519, Ferdinand Magellan set out on an expedition to the west. He sailed across the Atlantic and into the Pacific. He didn't fall off the edge of the world but rather was the first to sail all the way around it.

Later explorers discovered fabulous riches in the Americas. Gold, silver and gems found their way to Lisbon and then on to the Exchange in Antwerp. And exotic spices from the east were traded in the city of Antwerp too.

At the time when Abraham was born, the Seventeen Provinces of the Netherlands were under the control of the Holy Roman Emperor, Charles V, the King of Spain. Antwerp on the River Scheldt had become the great trading centre of the Netherlands, and one of the greatest in the whole world.

Each province of the country was like a separate state, having its own state council and constitution. Each organised its own affairs. We lived in a freedom that was greater than commonly enjoyed in most other parts of Europe.

Before this time, the Catholic Church had been dominant throughout western Europe. Both Charles V and later on his son, Philip II, were rabid protectors of Catholicism in their kingdom, largely through the workings of the Inquisition. In the Netherlands, more than thirteen hundred people were executed as heretics in Charles V's reign.

So not only was our world an exciting place to live in but it was also very dangerous. We had to be on our guard all the time, being careful what we said in public and who we said it to.

Martin Luther first posted his theses of belief on the church door at Wittenberg in 1517. It only took a few years before his ideas filtered into the Netherlands. Charles V acted with great hard-heartedness against those who were Lutheran. Philip II was even more rigorous.

But onto Abraham's story…

*

Mother always said that of signs or wonders at his birth on the fourth day of April in 1527 there were none. Well, what did she expect?

He was the firstborn child and only son of Leonard and Hannah Ortels. Mother adored her son from first sight. She said his birth was easy. After just five hours, it took one almighty push and he slid out like a slug.

Father wanted to name him Wilhelm after his grandfather but Mother thought he was more special than that. So Mother chose something grand from the Bible that would befit such a perfect little fellow: Abraham, the father of the chosen people, the wanderer through the desert, the one blessed with sons in his old age. Not that our Abe was blessed with these attributes.

Mother wondered who he would turn out like. Would he have the hard-nosed business head of his father, the successful merchant, or would he be of a gentler nature like his mother, the want-to-be painter.

Whichever, she was convinced that Antwerp was the best place to grow up in. It was the commercial centre of the whole world. Ships came and went from the bustling port bringing all sorts of goods to city shores. Foreigners from all lands and religions settled here. Fabulous riches came with being the business heart of Europe. Added to that, lots of painters, engravers and tapestry weavers produced their wares in the city.

'What more could you want?' Mother asked her little babe. 'You've got it all, my son. You'll go a long way, I'm sure of that.' She was always telling him to dream big dreams.

*

When we were still young children, there was a time that really terrified us. The fright of it imprinted itself indelibly on our minds for the rest of our lives.

Father and his brother-in-law, Jacob van Meteren, were intrigued by Protestant ideals and the faith of Martin Luther. Dare I say it, but many of Luther's ideals seemed to make much more sense than those of Catholics. Countless Catholic clerics lived such wanton lives and then believed that they could buy their way into heaven through indulgences. What a lot of rot! Luther preached that faith is the only necessity for salvation. Many in Antwerp were fully committed to the Lutheran way of thinking, despite the danger of the Catholic Inquisition that was imposed upon us by Spanish rulers in their efforts to get rid of every last Protestant, every last heretic.

Uncle Jacob worked as a publisher, printer and linguist at the time. Father had helped him secretly publish a Bible translated into the English language. Despite the danger, it was much safer to do this in Antwerp than in volatile London, where King Henry VIII was actively persecuting Catholics. Other Protestant books and works of Luther had been published in Antwerp for some time before this. But it had also been here in Antwerp that the first Protestant was burnt at the stake, becoming our first martyr. Then it all erupted: books and martyrs all consigned to the flames.

At the time, Father and Uncle Jacob were away in London trying to find suitable outlets for sales of their Bible.

A very loud banging on the front door put Mother on high alert.

'Go outside and play,' she whispered to us children, 'and keep your mouths tightly shut.'

While Elisabeth and I hid behind the cypress tree in the backyard,

Abraham stayed near the back door, shaking with fear and hoping to overhear what was going on.

Three large black-robed priests, like big black bears, were menacing Mother. 'We suspect that Protestants live in this place, and you know what that means.'

'No, no, you've got it entirely wrong.' Mother hoped that they would notice the large and gory crucifix and statue of the Virgin Mary on the mantelpiece. 'We are Catholics here, through and through.'

'Where is Leonard Ortels?' they demanded. 'We've come to arrest him on suspicion of heresy. And others of us have gone to arrest your kinsman, van Meteren.'

Mother was greatly alarmed, as she knew these people of the Inquisition were harsh and cruel.

They pushed roughly past her and started to empty shelves and trunks and scatter books and papers all over the floor. 'Looks like you're in the clear, this time,' they barked. 'Can't find anything suspicious-looking here,' and they stamped out of the room. 'We will be back sometime,' they said.

'What a relief.' said Mother. 'That was indeed a narrow escape.'

Abraham rushed into Mother's arms. Everyone began to breathe easily again.

But within the hour, there was another more timid knock at the door. It was a very pregnant Aunt Orillia van Meteren sobbing and trembling. She told a similar story of priests of the Inquisition at her house. 'I prayed to Almighty God,' she said, 'that they wouldn't find what they were searching for. And I promised God that if he protected me, I would mark his kindness by naming the child in my womb in honour of his deliverance.'

Although the searchers frequently laid their hands on the very chest that contained the hidden books, they didn't find them. So when Aunt Orillia's son was born, she named him Emanuel, a name that means God with us.

*

14

Abraham was only twelve when Father died, almost on the brink of manhood but still with much to learn.

Father had been feeling ill for weeks. He looked grey and wan. Such a terrible pain in his head and his gut. He hadn't been able to eat anything for two weeks.

We heard him talking to Mother. 'What will become of the children after I pass away? Ann and Elisabeth will be all right, they will find suitable husbands, but what of Abraham? At twelve, he's so earnest, yet at the same time he's a dreamer. He collects old coins and fragments of maps and frequents the docks talking to sailors who have come from journeys of exploration.' A rasping cough caused him to stop and catch his breath. 'And reading. He's always got his nose in a book. He likes to draw, not only pictures but maps too. He's got a real inclination for maps, has our Abe.'

'Yes, yes, I know all that,' said Mother, caressing what was left of his hair.

'Abraham needs to continue his education. The Classics, Latin and Greek, and mathematics: the foundations of humanism. He needs to be introduced to the whole gamut of humanism.' Another deep sigh followed by a great indrawing of breath. 'I'll see to it that Jacob becomes the children's guardian and supervises Abraham's learning.'

Mother nodded for these were her wishes for Abraham too.

'Then,' Father continued, 'after that, he should be old enough to take over my business that I hope you, my dearest Hannah, will look after while he's growing up.'

'I hope you've put all that in your will,' replied Mother.

As tears of grief spilled down our faces, Abraham could hardly see the spade when it was his turn to shovel the earth back into Father's grave. Father had been a good man and a loving father to all of us.

*

'Make sure Abraham continues with his education' were Father's parting words to Uncle Jacob van Meteren. And so it was.

Before he died, Father made sure that the three of us were well on our way to gaining an elementary education. We could all read and write fluently and calculate where calculations were needed. We were expected to read the recently printed Dutch Bible that was based on Luther's translations. Later, Abraham read the Latin Vulgate version, the only version authorised by the Catholic Church. We were encouraged to find out as much as we could about European countries and their history. This gave Abraham a great desire to go and see them all.

We learnt to play recorders and the lute, and to sing madrigals: a trio who were happy to entertain when called on. Mother introduced us to the world of art and took us to see works produced in Antwerp. The Lady Cathedral was an education in itself, especially the Last Supper portrayed in a stained-glass window. She encouraged us to draw and sketch all the time. Abraham could often be found down at the docks drawing ships and charts and the wide murky river itself.

Elisabeth and I were considered to have received enough learning by the age of twelve to last a lifetime but, being a boy, more was expected of Abraham.

'Lucky you!' We were envious.

'There's nothing to stop you from keeping on reading,' was his rejoinder.

It wasn't as if us girls didn't have a brain. It wasn't as if we couldn't go on to higher learning. It was just the custom that further education was only for boys. I decided then and there, by hook or by crook, to keep up with Abraham. However, I didn't care for mathematics.

Our younger van Meteren cousins joined our classes as they got old enough.

Sometimes Uncle Jacob, sometimes a tutor came to the house and directed the learning. The plan for Abe was a simple one. 'You must grasp the principles set out in Euclid's mathematical *Elements* and Ptolemy's *Geographica,* and you must be well-versed in basic Latin and Greek. Read all the classical authors from ancient Rome and Greece, and modern authors too, like Erasmus,' Uncle insisted.

Sometimes, it wasn't what Abraham actually learnt from these subjects that left a lasting impression. It was the underlying principles that became part of Abraham's being. Euclid stressed the importance of logical reasoning behind the proofs of his geometry. Thales proposed that all things could be explained in natural terms rather than as a result of supernatural or mythical happenings. Seneca advised that contentment is achieved through a simple, unruffled life that reflects nature and civic duty.

But it was most important to acquire the skills of speaking and writing persuasively. Verbal sparring at the dinner table gave us all lots of practice which stood us in good stead for adulthood. Cicero would have been proud of us.

Perhaps the most fundamental thing we all learnt was that learning didn't finish at the end of formal education. It is a lifelong pursuit, and that's what we did, especially Abraham. He spent the rest of his life learning; discovering the ins and outs of all sorts of things that he encountered in life. And I tried hard to keep up with him.

For Abe, the most exciting thing he learnt was that there were groups of people called humanists who studied the Classics for their relevance today. He wanted to join their conversations.

'You need to walk before you can run,' said Mother. 'Just wait until you're a little older to meet your humanists. It will happen soon enough.'

*

Before Father died, he had traded quite successfully in the antiquities business. After he died, Mother, who had always helped Father especially by keeping track of costs and payments, took over the running of the business. We children helped where we were able, at first running errands, delivering and fetching parcels large and small from people who did business with us.

As we grew older, Mother taught us a lot about where the pieces came from, who had owned them and what life was like in the times of their origin.

'You need to know the difference between Roman urns and Greek vases, between oil lamps from the Holy Land and those from Italy, and between Roman coins with emperors' heads and those with emblems of Roman legions,' she said.

Cleaning old objects was another skill we acquired. For coins and medallions, soapy water and a soft-bristle brush removed the surface dirt, and a good soak in oil softened any remaining encrustations. The process was then repeated until the greenish patina could be seen that formed on most ancient metal substances. We had to be very careful not to remove any of the patina, for that lessened the value of the coin. Abraham was fascinated by old coins and wasted no opportunity when delivering them to collectors to ask them about their value and their history. A lot of silver *denarii* and brass *sestertii* passed through our business, but only a few gold *aurei*.

It wasn't only coins that we dealt in. Ancient rings and bracelets, buckles and buttons, and other dress decorations that were small and made of metal, while occasionally a glass bead or two from ancient necklaces turned up. The ancient ladies certainly had a sense of taste in their dress.

Then there were pottery objects: vases and urns, plates and drinking cups, figurines and even busts, though Mother never accepted anything too big for us children to carry safely. Along with these old wares, Mother sold some new ones, especially glazed tiles that had recently begun to be produced in Delft.

'Those little white tin-glazed tiles painted with blue oxides are becoming very popular and will sell well,' she said. 'People really like their simple Dutch patterns.'

Old books were another item that were bought and sold.

'Surely I could keep one or two, Mother?' Abraham asked.

Printed books had only been produced for a little over a hundred years, so there weren't many of them. However, they were increasing in numbers all the time. Added to that, not many people could read foreign or ancient languages. Some books were very beautiful, with tooled leather binding. Occasionally, we came across a few single pages of hand-scribed illuminated manuscripts. Even though they had been removed from their original book, they sold well. They were often decorated with colourful patterns, tiny pictures or even gold leaf. As Abraham was learning both Latin and Greek at the time, he 'borrowed' any books in those languages and pored over them. Homer's tales of the battles of the Trojan War in the *Iliad* and the wanderings of Odysseus on his way home from war in the *Odyssey* always excited him. Abraham liked to read in Latin to us girls, especially Catullus's short poem about his lover's pet sparrow: *Passer mortuus est meae puellae, passer, deliciae meae puellae.* My lady's sparrow is dead, the sparrow which was my lady's delight.

'Bragger,' Elisabeth called him, even though we enjoyed his rendition.

And then there were the maps and navigation charts. Abraham first became interested in them when hanging about the docks as a young boy. He enjoyed watching the loading and unloading of cargoes and finding out where they came from. He loved the sounds of the port: the thrum of sail ropes against the masts of ships and the swish of water over the bows of barges, the grinding of the loading gear, the squawking of gulls and the yelling of masters in unknown languages. He liked the smell of the port: the murkiness of the river and the aroma of spices, from cloves to nutmegs and black peppercorns. Abraham would spend every spare minute down there on fine days; it was only a short walk from home.

Often, Mother would send me to fetch him home to do his tasks. 'Tell him to stop pestering the hard-working men down there and to get home at once.'

Abe's response to that was, 'Tell her to stop pestering me while I'm busy and not at all hungry.'

For Abe, the best part of visiting the dock area was talking to those sailors who could understand his tongue or his gestures. They'd tell him of their journeys hither and beyond. Some showed him their charts that

19

indicated where to sail in clear waters and where to avoid reefs, rocks and sand banks. Some had maps attached to their cabin walls, maps of their routes around the coast of Africa to the Indies, maps of coastlines of all the different parts of Europe, maps of anywhere and everywhere. It wasn't long before we were selling maps, old and new, in the business.

One day, Abraham came up with a brilliant idea: why not buy maps of paper or linen or vellum, then colour them and sell them again at twice the price?

'What a great plan,' said Mother. 'Let's try it.'

It wasn't long before the three of us were talented map illuminators and business was flourishing. Soon, it became a major part of family operations.

*

Abraham, Elisabeth and I started out as beginners in this map colouring business. But then we took it to a whole new level of expertise.

Abraham started travelling all over Europe to get hold of maps. He went in the company of other merchants as he was too young to go alone. He liked to beg, borrow or steal new, exciting and, if possible, valuable maps. He brought them back so that Elisabeth and I could mount them onto linen or canvas. Then we'd paint them and sell them for a profit. I took them to our own family stall at the marketplace and bargained with customers. Often, we served special clients who ordered how they wanted their maps coloured. These were good for business because we could charge higher prices.

Abraham showed us how to add ornaments to the maps to make them even more special. Ships with flags aflying sailed the oceans, monsters with hideous grins swam in the seas and gentle zephyrs blew from the cheeks of the winds.

We girls were best at this. We preferred to use the new pastel shades of colour. Bright colours are fine for paintings but softer pastels look better on maps. We felt like professional artists.

We ground our own pigments, then mixed them with water or linseed oil to make the paints. Ochre, umber and sienna tones smelled of the earth from which they came. The verdigris on copper made the green tones, while the blues came from azurite. Crushed malachite produced both green and blue tones. Black and white were the simplest colours to produce: white from chalk and black from charcoal. Chemical compounds yielded bright colours: white came from lead carbonate, orpiment yellow from arsenic sulphide, vermillion from mercuric sulphide, rust from iron oxide or old rusty bits of iron that could be found in the rubbish. You can see we had an eye for colour.

Elisabeth liked the action of the mortar and pestle to extract colours from plant materials: roots, stems, leaves and petals, or even from spices. Roots from the madder, a climbing plant with pretty yellow flowers, made a delicate pink shade; the pea flower, foliage of the indigo plant and woad leaves produced blue dyes; the spices turmeric and saffron yielded interesting yellow shades.

'But we couldn't afford the new carmine colour made from Mexican cochineal bugs,' Elisabeth liked to point out, 'nor the ultramarine from lapis lazuli. It was bad enough finding money for silver and gold leaf, which has to be hammered out very finely to stretch it further.' Elisabeth was fast learning Mother's financial skills.

Pastel colours were produced by mixing white lead with the colour pigments. Each time we mixed the same colour, it turned out a slightly different shade. It was always a surprise. We added variations of brown to hilly areas to create the illusion of undulating hillsides.

And if each of us coloured identical maps, we varied the colour scheme, so no two of the same map had the same appearance. Sometimes, they were totally different.

Elisabeth was forever worried about the expense of brushes used to apply the paints. We used brushes of mongoose hair for fine work, hog's bristle brushes for bolder strokes and, most costly of all, sable brushes of weasel's hair for larger smoother areas of colour.

And where did all of these exotic materials come from? Ships brought them from all over the world, and wagons arrived overland from all of

Europe and even beyond. There was a big market for paint bases in Antwerp, where the number of artists increased rapidly over the years. Buying painting materials from the local apothecary was my job.

We combined painting and illuminating with helping Mother continue the family business. Elisabeth and I did most of the painting while Abraham dealt in maps and books. Mother directed, and kept track of the money. Between us all, we made it work.

Elisabeth and I never tired of colouring maps. In fact, we often competed to see who produced the most pleasing colour combinations. Mother was the judge, but she was far too impartial and ascribed praise equally to both.

Hundreds of maps passed through our hands over the years.

*

Before any maps could be bought or sold, someone else had to have engraved them.

Abraham wasn't an engraver himself; later he employed others to do it for him. But he needed to be familiar with the procedures that he was asking his collaborators to carry out.

He thought it would be good for me to see the process too, not that I'd ever get the chance to try it, even if I wanted to, which I didn't.

'Would you like to come down to the engraving workshop with me?' asked Abraham. 'Hans Collaert, my apprentice friend, has offered to show us around his place. It's small and cramped but I guess we'll fit in. We're both pretty slim.'

Engraving on copper plates for printing wasn't an easy art. It was a specialised skill that took a long time to master in all of its intricacies.

'As you can see,' said Hans, pointing to a number of boys in the workshop, 'engraving is done on a polished copper plate that sits on a cushion so that it can easily be turned. Beating and polishing come first. We begin with a grinding stone and water to do the polishing. That's a messy business. Next comes pumice stone, then hardened charcoal followed by a steel burnisher.'

'I can see that the final result is a beautifully smooth surface,' I said.

Taking a burin and cradling it like an apple in his hand, Hans continued, 'The basic tool of an engraver is the burin. Getting it right is what we aim for, but it takes years of practice to incise perfect lines. It's a simple tool really, but in the hands of the right person it can do wonders. I'm but a beginner in the art.' He screwed the shaft to the stem of the mushroom-shaped handle and explained, 'This allows the angle of the shaft to be varied for different processes. It is important to keep the cutting edge sharp all the time. More than once, I've nearly cut off my finger when the burin has slipped. There was blood everywhere.'

'Ouch,' interjected Abraham. 'It sounds like there could now be several engravers with the top of a finger missing.'

Hans nodded and grinned. 'You support the head of the burin in the palm of your hand, then the index and middle finger guide the shaft. It's like a plough in the earth, making a furrow in the same way that a plough turns the soil of a field.' He demonstrated the action. 'You have to work away from the body and use a combination of hand pressure and movement of the copper plate to make regular lines. Believe me, it takes a lot of concentration to push the burin through the metal for long periods of time.'

Then Hans showed us a variety of other tools that made lines look different. Thick lines and thin lines. The deeper the cut, the darker the line.

'You have to be very careful for the slightest scratch on the copper plate will print as a fine black line,' he said.

'That could be hard to get rid of,' said Abraham.

'What's that young man over there doing?' I asked.

'He's creating half-tones and shadows by hatching and cross-hatching. And in the corner by the window is an apprentice who is producing a stippled effect by punching the burin into the copper plate.'

Hans puffed out his chest. 'I'm nearly up to learning to engrave text, both Gothic and italic,' he boasted.

'I quite like the look of the smooth-flowing italic. I've noticed that it's becoming fashionable now,' said Abraham.

'And much easier to read,' I added.

'It's easier to engrave too,' replied Hans. 'And here's the really difficult part about any engraving: the final image is the reverse of what is incised on the plate. So you have to keep your wits about you especially when cutting italic lettering. You always have to think what it looks like in reverse; in *intaglio*. They call it mirror-image engraving.'

'How long does an engraved plate last?' asked Abraham. 'Doesn't it become worn out eventually?'

'It will make many, many prints,' replied Hans, 'but you're right, they do become worn eventually, and a new one has to be made.'

We were amazed at the number of different images that could be produced by a combination of all these tools and methods.

Abraham could envisage illustrations for books, maps and charts, prints for their own worth and reproductions of artists' paintings. 'So an engraver has to have a sense of pleasing design as well,' he commented. 'It's no wonder that your apprenticeship is for five years.'

*

'The next step in the engraving process is printing,' Abraham explained the next day. 'While printing in itself is a completely separate art, the engraver has to know how it works in order to do his job properly. I don't suppose you would like to come over to Plantin's with me,' he asked.

It wasn't far, so we walked over to the workshop. Plantin agreed to show us his printing set-up and explained that the art of printing had two separate components: the production of typefaces to create the text, and the printing process itself.

'The separate typeface pieces come in individual letters or groups of commonly twinned letters and are made from a lead-based alloy,' he said. 'They are cast in hand moulds that we printers call matrices. I like to use the French Garamond typefaces. I have to lay out the letters in rows, and the rows on the pages ready for printing.'

'It all sounds like slow and painstaking work,' I said.

Next we inspected the printing press, a large contraption which transferred an image from a prepared inked surface to a receiving surface, like paper or cloth.

'Look closely, Ann,' said Plantin, 'and you'll see that when ink is applied to the copper plate, it spreads into the incised lines. We wipe off the excess ink so that it remains in the engraved furrows and not on the plate itself.'

He showed us how a frame containing the inked copper plate is placed under another frame containing paper that is screwed down by a hand-held lever. On the outer side of the two frames are layers of felt for protection from the press itself. Then all is rolled through the heavy press. Under pressure, damp paper is forced into the ink furrows so that the image emerges on the paper.

'A man could develop a good set of muscles as he forces the roller into contact with the paper,' said Abraham.

'Indeed,' agreed Plantin, flexing his upper arm to illustrate.

Plantin told us that he had several presses to begin with; the number grew with the success of his business.

'Is paper easy to come by?' asked Abraham.

'It is,' replied Plantin. 'Much of it is made in Italy, Germany or France and distributed through Antwerp. The specialty paper, vellum, is made from the hide of cows in the countryside around our city.'

'And what about ink?' I added.

'Oil-based ink is made from a mixture of turpentine, lampblack and linseed oil, so handling it is a dirty job. The ink is applied in a circular motion using dabbers: leather balls stuffed with wool or horsehair. With ink-based oils the paper can be dry, in which case the image has more contrast, or the paper can be damp, in which case the image has a much greater range of tones.'

'The acrid smell of turpentine and the loud clank of the printing presses that waft out of the print room are quite overpowering,' said Abraham, screwing up his nose.

'Constant exposure to acids, solvents and vapours used in the printing process can considerably shorten a printer's life, if he is not very careful,' said Plantin. 'I, on the other hand, am a careful man.'

And lastly we learnt that illustrations needed to be added. Fancy initial letters were often designed and coloured by calligraphers and illuminators.

'I prefer engraved copperplate illustrations rather than the older woodcuts,' said Plantin.

'I guess that sometimes with maps, a page needs two pressings, one using the typefaces for the text, the other using the copperplate for the illustrations,' ventured Abraham.

When the printing was finished, the sheets of paper were weighted down to keep them flat while they dried. Looking around the workshop, we noticed individually printed sheets hanging in lines for a final airing.

Then Plantin showed us how the separate pages are bound into books ready for sale. I've heard that Plantin became quite famous for his beautiful inlaid bindings and book covers.

'I believe many say that sometimes your books are excessively decorated and feature every peculiarity of typography,' said Abraham with a smile.

Affronted, Plantin replied, 'I've always taken a great deal of pride in the quality and accuracy of my work. I even hang the galley proofs in front of my workshop and offer a reward to anyone who can find faults in the text. Scholars from all over Europe come to me in Antwerp to have their writings published at the House of Plantin.'

We realised that a printer has to employ many people for different aspects of the process: typesetters, engravers, pressers, proofreaders, binders and sundry labourers. Plantin told us that he left the distribution of finished books to others. Nowadays, he sells many at the Frankfurt Book Fair.

*

Later at home, as Abraham and I sat around the fire, finishing our ale, Abraham told me about an earlier Antwerpian printer, Hieronymus

Cock, who was also a fine painter of elegant landscapes. In 1548, he had set up his own publishing house, Aux Quatre Vents.

'You can see from its name that he had big ideas even then of distributing engravings, etchings and paintings all over the world, to the four winds. He started out by printing a series of etchings of Roman ruins that he did at the time of his early visit to Rome to learn from the masters.'

'Ah, they all went to Rome early in their careers,' I said.

'Gradually, Cock changed printmaking from doing it all himself into a whole industry based on many workers,' said Abraham. 'He reproduced designs by famous Italian masters as well as famous Dutch and Flemish artists. He even printed maps. He made many, many prints of Peter Bruegel's works; they sold like hot bread. Bruegel's *Twelve Large Landscapes*, mainly scenic mountain views, were especially popular. He distributed the prints far and wide, even as far as South America and Japan, and began to make a name for himself. His richly patterned and ermine-trimmed doublet spoke of his financial success. He operated one of the most important printing houses in Europe in those early times of printing. However, that was before Plantin came along and took over his position, doing bigger and better things.'

'But surely Antwerp is large enough for several high-class printers.' I said. I had heard a lot of that before and had even met his wife, Diericx. Cock liked to call her his dear and beautiful one with the glorious nose and the trim little waist. 'Didn't she use to work alongside him?' I asked.

'She did indeed, and she did far more than provide drinks for the workers. She was an expert with the accounts and knew every aspect of the business.'

Ah yes, I thought, some women in this world manage to make opportunities for themselves beyond the domestic scene.

We then played a game of chess which, for once, I won.

*

'I wanted to tell you more about Christopher Plantin,' said Abraham as we were mixing paints one day. 'He first came to Antwerp to avoid the Spanish Inquisition in France. It had already condemned one printer to the fire there for the heresy of producing forbidden books that may have cast aspersions on the Catholic Church and its beliefs. I was just twenty-one when Plantin set up shop as a bookbinder and leather-worker in Antwerp. After seven years of binding and seeing the opportunities provided by this great city of books and learning, Plantin turned to the printing trade and produced and published scholarly books of every kind. He was always meticulous in his work. His clothes, always in the height of fashion, reflected his professionalism, He liked his starched ruffs folded in a figure-of-eight style.'

'It must have taken his wife hours to press them,' I said. 'She's got one of those new hot-box irons. I like the thought of them.'

'Plantin is a gentleman who lets little sway him from his course in life,' Abraham continued. 'In Antwerp, he found easy access to materials, abundant craftsmen and accessible markets. What more could he want as a printer?'

'Plantin has had some close encounters with the Inquisition, hasn't he?' I said. 'It seemed as though the Inquisition was keeping an eye on him.'

'In 1562, he was suspected of heresy and had to flee Antwerp for a couple of years. When the Spanish tried to sell off his presses and other equipment after his escape, his friends bought them back for him. That's how highly they thought of him. He returned to Antwerp a couple of years after that and then later, in 1576, set up a new shop at the Vrijdagmarkt under the sign of De Gulden Passer, the Golden Compass. That's where we were the other day.'

The Golden Compass is a complex of workshops and offices with a house adjoining it. Every Friday, come rain or shine, in the marketplace, the excited cries of sellers and buyers haggling for better prices for their wares rises up through the windows.

'He uses the sign of the compass as the focal point for his printer's mark.' Abraham got up to fetch one of Plantin's volumes to illustrate his point. 'On the vignette on the back page of this book is a compass, a few angels and the motto *Labore et constantia*. By hard work and tenacity. These are the things that defined his life as a publisher.'

'I like the symbolism of the compass,' I said, 'with its still point and its circling point.'

'It is also an accurate tool for a draughtsman as he draws up plans,' Abraham added.

I know that Plantin's roomy house was often the venue for gatherings of the humanist circle that both he and Abraham belong to. Discussion would sometimes go on into the middle of the night, especially when interesting and learned visitors happened to be in town.

I also know how highly Abraham considered Plantin. They became close friends, regularly sharing a beer in the evening. We would often join his family for a meal, and they'd return the compliment.

*

Belonging to a guild is important for most artists and craftspersons. There are guilds for all sorts of groups in Antwerp. Each has their own guild house in the Grote Markt near the Lady Cathedral. Beside St Luke's are the guilds of wine merchants, crossbowmen and bricklayers each have their own statues on top of step-gabled roofs. A golden fox keeps an eye on the traders and a golden eagle hovers over the grocers.

Abraham was twenty-one when, in 1548, he joined the guild as an *afsetter van karten*, a colourer of maps. The Guild of St Luke was the guild for painters, manuscript illuminators, art dealers, and the like. It had a market stall in front of the cathedral for selling paintings.

Abraham explained, 'Once registered with a particular guild, a craftsperson works under a master for several years until he has completed the entrance requirements. Then he pays a fee and produces a masterpiece. This enables him to become a free master and work for any guild member or for himself. After that, artists can sell their own works, set up their own workshop with apprentices, and sell the work of other artists. Guild membership also offers a sort of protection

against painters from other areas and gives judgements on disputes between artists or between artists and clients. You could have joined the
Guild of St Luke too,' said Abraham. 'You are probably a more efficient
map colourer than I am.'

I know a couple of women who have entered guilds. But you wouldn't
catch me joining one, for it means a time of living at the master's house
for some years. That could be a source of potential problems!

When people entered the Guild of St Luke, they often took on a
Latinised version of their name. Thus my brother became known as
Ortelius.

One of the benefits of joining St Luke's was that he got to know
other members of the guild, especially artists, engravers and printers.
He was delighted to find that many of them were humanists. It wasn't
long before he joined their circle.

*

I know how besotted Abraham was with maps. There was a time much
later when he went to Hieronymus Cock's workshop to check on
progress of a large wall map of America that Cock was producing with
the Spanish cartographer Diego Gutiérrez. That was in 1562.

Abraham couldn't wait to share his excitement about that map. 'The
map is of America, the newest part of the world,' he told me. 'It was
made on six separately engraved sheets, by far and away the largest
printed map of America in existence. The map was printed here in
Antwerp because the Spanish didn't have the skills to print such a complicated thing.'

Gutierrez told him that nobody knew much about the interior of
the American continent, so he filled it with settlements, rivers and
mountains, along with lots of parrots and monkeys. 'And I included
some Brazilian cannibals and Patagonian giants, and even an erupting
volcano in central Mexico.' he said.

I did so admire the mermaids and huge sea creatures in the surrounding seas.

It was indeed a complex map. But it was the first to show the Californian coast and the Amazon River. What I liked was the image of the Spanish King Philip in his chariot with Poseidon crossing the Atlantic to claim America.

'What a pretentious man we have for a king,' said Abraham with a chuckle.

*

There was a special day of celebration in our city in early 1549. The city hosted a triumphal entry when Charles V brought his son and heir, Prince Philip of Spain, to meet our people. Peter Coecke van Aelst was in charge of the spectacular decorations for the royal entry.

Van Aelst was an artist in many mediums and quite flamboyant in style. Those two qualities made an ideal combination for a leader of such an enterprise. He did painting, woodcuts, tapestries, sculpture, and architectural and stained-glass design. And he liked to wear a red beret in the manner of French painters. Red was his favourite colour.

Abraham explained that much earlier, van Aelst had travelled to Constantinople in an attempt to establish business connections for his tapestries. 'The trip was a failure,' he said. 'However, one of its outcomes was that Van Aelst often appeared in Turkish costume, with a long flowing robe, loose baggy trousers and high boots, crowned with a red turban.'

'So I guess that he was a figure who stood out from the crowd,' I said.

The triumphal entry was a grand spectacle. Without a doubt, the power and loyalty of our city were on display.

Van Aelst engaged many artists and workmen to put it all together, including his apprentice Peter Bruegel. He even found painting jobs for Abraham.

The triumphal road into the city was lined with columns, decorated with festoons and interspersed with flaming torches. There were two huge triumphal arches, one each for King Charles V and Prince Philip, with their statues on the top. More than two thousand other columns were painted.

It was good that van Aelst finished constructing the sculpture *Giant of Antwerp* in time for the celebrations.

'It was a huge undertaking,' Abraham said. 'He also published a commemorative souvenir with woodcut illustrations.'

We heard later that the burgomeister and his statesmen met the king and prince at the city gate and led them in procession into the city. The procession was headed by noisy musicians with their trumpets, drums and shawms, accompanied by four thousand Dutch soldiers marching with their banners held high. The royal visitors watched tournaments and jousts before retiring for a prodigious feast, accompanied by the best musicians that Antwerp could offer.

The day was declared a holiday so that everyone could partake in the celebration. Our family waved and cheered and enjoyed the spectacle as it passed our house.

On that day, van Aelst tossed a long and vibrant red cloak over his shoulders.

'It was just a pity that it rained on his spectacle,' said Abraham.

All of that happened while the Spanish kings were still reasonably friendly with us people of Antwerp, before they got so heavy-handed and oppressive.

*

About this time too, Charles V established the Seventeen Provinces of the Netherlands as separate from the Holy Roman Empire and separate from France, but still under his rule.

2

One of the first people Abraham met through the Guild of St Luke was the painter Peter Bruegel. They became good friends.

When I first met him, he was an apprenticed to Peter Coecke van Aelst and became a master in the painters' Guild of St Luke. Like many upcoming painters, he spent a couple of years in that great melting pot of art, Italy, and especially Rome. He went to have a look at what was happening in the painting world there. And on the way he passed over the majestic Alps of Switzerland. Vistas of snow-covered mountain tops which he said took his breath away. He felt impelled to stop and capture the scene on canvas. It was during this trip that he developed a distinctive style of landscape painting which he used later in many works. Sometimes, only a little of the landscape appeared in the background, through an archway or a window. I loved those bits.

He took Abraham along with him. His eyes twinkled with excitement as he regaled me with stories of his time there.

They left on horseback in early summer with the sun on their faces. They travelled with a merchants' convoy for protection, and spent the nights in wayside inns.

'Ah, for a blazing log and a frothing beer,' Abraham sighed, after a long day's ride. 'A nice hot soak would be good for my aching limbs, too.'

Next morning, while they were eating their stale crusts, Bruegel grizzled, 'I can't say that I enjoyed the bed bugs that spent the night running between the rough blankets.'

'His unruly hair always looked as though bugs had built a nest in it,' I commented.

Bruegel proved to be an affable companion. However, Abraham was more interested in antiquities from ancient Roman civilisation than in paintings.

Together, they visited the Hippodrome of Domitian, a stadium for horse and chariot racing.

'I'd read about this place,' said Abraham. 'They call it Circus Maximus. It could seat thousands of people along the banks of its long sides. How the ancient Romans loved their horse racing and shouted and cheered on top note. In those days, chariots pulled by two or four horses would race around the course seven times, rounding the tight turning post at the narrow semicircular ends. I can almost hear the people cheering with great excitement as the chariots jostled for space when they rounded the post all at the one time.'

'And I'd imagine that more often than not they'd crash in a heap of injured horses and charioteers.' Bruegel gesticulated wildly to make his point.

'It's a cruel way to treat a horse,' said Abraham. 'I'm glad that sport hasn't stood the test of time.'

Abraham bought a few old Roman coins. Doesn't he always? Some were from the era of the republic. As well, he picked up several small antiquities to bring home for the business, including a small pottery oil lamp and a bronze ring with an agate stone. He thought he'd better not take the little glass flask; it might break on the journey home.

'More's the pity, for it sounds very attractive and would have fetched a good price,' I said.

They took a day trip to Solfatara near Naples, where there was a dormant volcano that emitted foul-smelling jets of sulphurous steam from its bowels. They scrambled down its steep inside to the crater at the bottom. Bruegel lost his footing on a sloping patch of scree but landed on the floor with a bump.

Abraham went to explore the steaming fumaroles and bubbling mud pools. Suddenly, a strong jet of hissing steam escaped with a whoosh that nearly knocked him over.

'Watch out, be careful, you oaf,' shouted Bruegel. He could hardly be heard over the constant bubbling of the thick black water in the mud pools.

'How this stuff stinks!' Abraham turned up his nose in disgust.

'And to think you nearly fell into that large hole, so keen were you to see what all that yellow crust on the rocks was.' Bruegel laughed.

'Good thing I didn't. I might have ended up like a cooked lobster.'

Of course, Bruegel spent time with famous Italian painters, learning their techniques which he later adapted to his own style. And of course, too, Abraham went along with him to see the wondrous works of Michelangelo on the Sistine Chapel ceiling.

After a couple of weeks, Abraham was reluctant to leave Bruegel and Rome to return to Antwerp with a party of other travellers.

When Bruegel got back to Antwerp, he worked for a long time with Hieronymus Cock in his publishing house, the Four Winds. There he produced prints on a whole range of subjects.

He often came to eat the evening meal with us and would elaborate on his latest works. He made over forty designs for engravings in the fantastical and pessimistic drawing style that was becoming popular.

'They are often quite satirical in nature,' Bruegel explained. 'Some might call them imaginative while others call them grotesque. But there is a good market for them and, like the rest of us, I have to pay the rent and eat.'

I didn't like them, but I refrained from telling Bruegel so.

There were many painters who worked in Antwerp at this time, but Bruegel seemed to have success. 'People like my work. I sold a lot.'

He was fortunate enough to gradually acquire many wealthy patrons who encouraged him, purchased his paintings and became friends. Both Christopher Plantin and Abraham had bought one of his paintings. We had Bruegel's *Death of a Virgin* hanging in our house. I liked the way the contrast between dark and light is highlighted in that painting. It's almost as if the virgin is so fully in the light that she might already be in paradise.

Abraham told me that Bruegel often went along to the humanist circle and joined the discussions and arguments. 'As a painter, he offered a unique perspective on what it means to be human. He often portrayed ordinary peasants doing ordinary things, like dancing, robbing a bird's nest or resting under a tree. I like the innovation of those works.'

Bruegel was nearly forty when he married Mayken. He said, 'We went to live in Brussels because my mother-in-law insisted that I be beyond the reach of my former lover.'

Peter and Mayken had two sons, Peter and Jan. But he still kept in touch with his friends, often visiting us in Antwerp, for Brussels is not far away.

*

Martin de Vos was another friend of Abraham from the Guild who spent a lot of time at our place. He too went to Italy on the back of a horse when he was young to further his painting techniques by learning from Italian masters.

De Vos was enchanted with Rome, with the brilliant artworks produced not only in his time, but also in ancient times. 'All the remnants of ancient Rome,' he exclaimed, 'the Colosseum, the Forum, and the temples: such glorious architecture. I do so like the Temple of the Vestal Virgins and the Temple of Caesar.'

When de Vos got back to Antwerp, he started a circle for Romophiles.

'What are they?' I asked.

'Lovers of Rome, what else?' said Abraham. 'Only those who have been to Rome can belong to his Romanist circle. We meet occasionally to keep ourselves up to date on news from Rome, whether it's new painters, recent paintings or lately discovered antiquities.'

'I suppose that as humanists you appreciate all things classical that come from Rome,' I retorted.

'Sometimes I go along to the Romanists' gatherings. As you know, I can get carried away with Roman coins and what they reveal of ancient Roman times,' said Abraham.

'I can well imagine that,' I said.

Keeping up with the latest in Roman archaeology was another of Abraham's favourite pastimes. He liked to dig deep to find traces of past cultures and understand their meanings. He often said that all Roman roads led to Rome and that many parts of them were still in existence. He ought to have known; he had travelled on *mijls* of them.

*

From early in his business life, Abraham went to the Frankfurt Book Fair in Germany each year to sell books, both on his own behalf and for others. Cartloads of them. Whenever he could get away at the time of the fairs, he would head for Frankfurt, even until he was quite old.

The twice-yearly Frankfurt Book Fairs were famous. While Frankfurt had been a market town for centuries, its book fair was barely a hundred years old. People came from all over Europe. They came by boat down the River Main, by ox cart with merchants across the countryside, and on foot from nearer places.

Frankfurt was a great publishing centre. Many people from professions associated with books gathered in Frankfurt for the fair, so it was a place where discussions were held with writers and scholars, publishers and printers, and typesetters and binders. How Abraham relished such conversations. He learnt much from the huge variety of interesting people in Frankfurt at the time.

Anyone interested in the printed word went along, some to sell or barter, others to buy or barter, some just to marvel at the great variety of books there. The classics could be found alongside accounts of voyages to the ends of the earth.

'I've seen accounts there written by Columbus and Vespucci about their explorations in the New World. And even charts of China by Marco Polo. It is a rare thing thing to come by such treasures,' said Abraham.

I went with him one year and what a treat it was. I didn't get to leave Antwerp very often.

Church bells announced the beginning of the day's trading, from half past eleven in the morning until sundown. It was all hustle and bustle. There were hundreds of people there moving from one stall to another in an unending throng.

All sorts of noisy people were there. I enjoyed the musicians and meistersingers, but stayed clear of the fortune tellers. Acrobats and conjurers did their tricks on every corner. Harlots flouted their wares and beggars their empty bowls. What's the world coming to that poor people have to go to such lengths to earn a coin?

In addition to books, goods from all over the world were for sale. There were aromatic spices and dried herbs, pungent wursts and aged wine, and tapestries and cloths with intricate designs. A feast for the senses. The perfect place to buy something special to take home to Mother and Elisabeth. Frankfurt had once been a Roman town, so Abraham was always on the look out for old coins and other antiquities.

As well as filling orders for others, Abraham bought books for his growing collection from learned authors both recent and old. Most importantly, he purchased dozens of maps that he took home for me and Elisabeth to delicately paint before selling them on.

I helped him set up a stall there, selling and buying books for printers and publishers that he knew in Antwerp. Later, Plantin would keep a permanent storehouse in Frankfurt to save on his annual cartage to and fro. Then as Plantin got busier with both printing and distribution, Abraham would do his business for him, for a commission of course. He sent books home from the fair packed in crates and loaded on boats for the journey back to Antwerp.

Every day that we were there, we spent some time in conversation with other dealers in books and maps. And often their wives were with them. I found myself particularly drawn to a fresh-faced, well-dressed fellow sitting opposite me. I couldn't keep my eyes from his comely frame with its red velvet doublet and matching hose.

At first he didn't notice me, then suddenly he turned his attention to me and started an intelligent conversation. I thought to myself I wouldn't mind getting to know him better. But we had to return to Antwerp the next day.

*

It was in Frankfurt in 1554 that Ortelius first met Gerard Mercator, who was to become such an excellent friend and mentor. Over several evenings with a beer and meal in an inn, they shared their stories. From what I knew of Mercator, I could well imagine the conversation.

'When I first came to Antwerp, Ortelius, you were only a child. I graduated from the university at Leuven in 1532 and changed my name from Gerhard de Kremer to its Latin form of Gerardus Mercator.'

'What were you studying in Leuven?' Abraham asked.

'Philosophy and its thoughts and ideals,' he answered, as if that was the only thing to study at university. 'But at the time I was having trouble making sense of the biblical account of the origin of the universe compared to that of Aristotle. I began to have doubts about what philosophers really knew about the concept of truth. So I decided not to continue at university but instead went travelling to a number of places including Antwerp. I didn't know of course that you lived there at that time.'

'And any time you come, you know you can find a bed at my house,' Abraham quickly assured him.

'Thanks,' he said. 'I'll take you up on that some day. But, moving on, I was hoping that by my travels I would avoid interrogation about my religious beliefs, as the Spanish seemed to be checking on all university students to make sure that they followed Catholic ideology.'

'You're not alone there. They check anyone interested in acquiring knowledge or passing on learning,' Abraham grimaced, remembering Father's experience with the Inquisition

'Travelling got me interested in geography,' Mercator continued. 'I began to see it could be the subject to best explain the structure of the world which God created. Then I returned to Leuven, where I married my Barbara and had my first child. I set myself up there as a cartographer, and an instrument and globe maker.'

Now Abraham was really interested. 'Do you think I could buy one of your middle-sized globes? The terrestrial type, not a celestial one. It would surely look good in my study.'

'Well, certainly I'll do my best.' Mercator went on, 'I was twenty-five when I drew and engraved my first map; it was of Palestine. In 1538, I produced a map of the world, followed a couple of years later by a map of Flanders. I supervised the surveying of that myself. It was painstaking work completing all that drafting and engraving. I like to be quite accurate, you know, but it slows me up sometimes. But,' and here Mercator's voice started to quiver somewhat, 'the Spanish Inquisition caught up with me and charged me with Lutheran heresy in 1544. It was partly because of my Protestant beliefs that I didn't tell them about, but I suppose it was also due to the fact that I travelled so widely to get information for my maps that their suspicions were aroused. I was imprisoned for seven long months in Rupelmonde castle, seven months with nothing to do except to dwell on what it was doing to my young family. I had to reassess again and again my own beliefs.'

'How demoralising,' Abraham said. 'How did you get out of that?'

'Nothing was found to connect me with the others arrested at the same time, even after they had been tortured for information about me. They searched my house and took my belongings but eventually found nothing incriminating to show that I was anything but a good Catholic. There were forty-two others arrested with me. Two of them were burned at the stake, one was beheaded and one woman was buried alive. It was horrendous.' He shuddered even as he spoke. 'The putrid smell of burning flesh and the dreadful groans of the buried woman. You could hear it even as they were piling the dirt on top of her. They stayed in my nightmares for many long years.'

'Enough of that. Stop!' Abraham cried, for he couldn't bear stories of torture and death.

'Well, that's how it was, horrible and all! Thank goodness for the parish priest and the head of the university, who between them made sure that the charges against me were dropped; so I got out of it with my skin intact and my head still on my neck.'

'My God, that was close. You must have been terrified as well as being tremendously brave,' Abraham said, thinking that it was no wonder that Mercator's long dour face and bushy eyebrows were those of a worried man.

Mercator continued his story. 'After my release, I returned to my family in Leuven. I was forced to pay for the cost of my own imprisonment, so I had to work twice as hard to make a living for both myself and my family. Anyway, I decided that it still wasn't really safe to stay in Leuven, so I moved my family just over the border to Duisburg in Germany in 1552, where people were more accepting of Protestants. Of course, I hadn't been Catholic for some time. It was at Duisburg that I opened a workshop and made maps of Europe and the British Isles as well as many others.'

'I'll have to visit sometime, because, as you know by now, maps are my passion too.' Abraham was looking for an invitation. It came forth and was eagerly accepted.

*

During the end of 1559 and early into 1560, Abraham spent some months travelling to France with a group of friends. At the outset, Abe pulled his knee-high hiking boots on over thick woollen hose and tightened the laces around the buttons up the side. The boots had done many years of service and so were quite discoloured. However, I kept them polished for him, under his instructions as to the degree of shine, for he was fussy about what he wore.

It was cold, but they were wrapped in plenty of clothes and took their gloves and blankets. Abraham was looking forward to a holiday with good companions, but he and Gerard Mercator were also looking for maps and other old artefacts. Abe kept a record of this journey and let me read it when he got home. It was very wordy and full of detail. It took me a week to get it read. Some excerpts follow.

Passing through hilly woodlands, grassy plains and fertile farmlands, we all enjoyed the scenery as we travelled on barges on rivers and canals that meandered through the countryside. It turned out to be a series of short trips as a weary horse trudged along the bank pulling a loaded barge: a journey designed to rest the body and refresh the soul. Mercator, Frans Hogenberg and Johannes Sadlier and I had plenty of time to relax and laugh together.

'Ah, this the life,' I said, 'we should do more of this.'

On the way, we visited Trier, or Augusta Treverum as the Romans had called it. It was west of the Rhine in Germany. There still remained a huge fortified gateway, Porta Nigra, set in what had been Roman defensive walls.

There were other ruins of Roman architecture there too, including a bathing complex and a mint. But most exciting were the remains of an amphitheatre that was so big it could seat thirty thousand spectators. It was here that Constantine once had several thousand Franks and Bructeri butchered for public amusement. I'm glad those times have passed.

Some of our group immediately gave an impromptu rendition of what went on in the amphitheatres: roaring like lions, and whipping, yelling and groaning like gladiators. Rolling with laughter, we could certainly imagine the scenes of snarling lions and gladiators tearing each other up. However, Mercator and I refrained from such goings on. It's one thing to act out such barbarian behaviour but quite another to joke about it. To think that people went along to such inhumane spectacles for entertainment.

On top of the hill in Trier was a palace that Constantine had built in the fourth century that eventually became a basilica with a huge hall. It was originally fitted with a hypocaust.

'What on earth's a hypocaust?' asked Hogenberg, his eyes twinkling beneath bushy brows.

'It's a floor and wall heating system,' I explained. 'The floor was on a layer of concrete raised above the ground by stubby pillars. Hot air from the furnace below would pass through spaces under the floor and inside the walls.'

'Pity the poor Roman slave constantly loading wood into the furnace to keep it going,' said Sadlier. 'Or worse yet, cutting the timber to start with.'

'But those Romans were certainly innovative,' added Mercator.

We walked along a network of Roman roads, long and straight. I explained the intricate and labour-intensive process by which the

Romans built their roads. They dug a wide level-bottomed ditch, filled it with small stones and sand, then laid large flat stones on the top so that they fitted together closely. That resulted in a level surface and long lasting roads. A bridle path for horses ran along the edge of the road.

We soon came to the district of Lorraine, where we saw an almost perfect old aqueduct that had brought water from far away. What a thing of beauty and symmetry as it crosses deep valleys.

At Poitiers in France, we met up with friends from Antwerp, Philip Galle and Joris Hoefnagel. We took some red wine, soft cheese and ripe pears out to the Pierre Levée, a famous megalith. Originally a cover for an ancient burial chamber, it had lately become an attraction for sightseers. We all carved our names in Latin on the large slab of rock, balanced on four stone legs. All the visitors did it, their names inscribed for all posterity.

'It looks like a giant table covered in graffiti,' remarked Hogenberg.

'I could paint a picture of this,' said Hoefnagel.

Poitiers was an interesting place in the eyes of a historian. Here was another Roman amphitheatre and another Roman aqueduct. It was also the place where the English Black Prince Edward defeated the French in a battle two hundred years ago. It had a beautiful old church.

'What city doesn't?' retorted Sadlier.

We were impressed by the size of some very old buildings in Poitiers. A castle and extensive fortifications, a cathedral and wealthy abbeys, royal courts and a university, all needed exploring. We also visited printing shops and discovered bustling markets. I only bought a couple of maps from the bookstall, haggling didn't do much to bring the price down.

Poitiers was where François Rabelais, a renowned writer and humanist, had lived. I've read some of his works. He used his spare time to write and publish humorous pamphlets which were critical of both the church and state authority. I'm taken with his saying, 'A bellyful is a bellyful.'

Mercator added, 'Some of those books were placed on the index of banned books by the Catholic Church, and you know what that means.'

Many of his works were satirical, many of them bawdy. Rabelais aimed his commentaries at those in authority, for he was a keen observer of events that unfolded during the first half of our century.

'He died not long ago, didn't he?' asked Sadlier.

Hogenberg nodded. 'And reportedly his last words were, "I go to seek the Great Perhaps." What a man!'

Then we headed to Paris. How pleasant it was to wander along the banks of the grey and muddy Seine with its river traffic: boats carrying goods, barges loaded with coal, small boats carrying people, and sailing ships with goods for hither and beyond. We wandered until we reached Notre Dame cathedral with its flying buttresses and delicate carvings of biblical stories around the doorway.

'So that illiterate people could get their share of the Bible,' remarked Hogenberg.

'But that's not why we came to Paris at all,' interrupted Mercator. 'There is a narrow, cobbled street along the Left Bank where itinerant booksellers set up their stalls. All sorts of books, almanacs, maps and charts, and even the odd Roman coin or two, are sold for a song. Plantin once had a bindery and bookshop here in Paris. It was he who told us about this place. You won't be able to keep Ortelius away from it.'

He was right, I spent a good hour there.

Later, we climbed Montmartre to see the city below.

'*Voila*, I give you Paris,' I threw open my arms in an exaggerated salute. 'There were once Roman temples at the top of this hill, one for Mars, the god of war, and one for Mercury, the god of trade.'

'That's just about the sum of our world today: bloody wars and lucrative trade,' muttered Hogenberg.

'It was here too, not so long ago,' I added, 'that Ignatius of Loyola started the order of Jesuits when he and a small group of men took their vows of poverty, chastity and obedience in the church of St Pierre on Montmartre. One of his first followers, Francis Xavier, sailed to India as a missionary and travelled further to the east. He used to send me maps of those parts, through the Jesuits in Antwerp.'

While we were in all those places, I met and made friends with some experts of the cartography world, not to mention numismatic and antiquarian experts.

Abraham told me that it was on that journey that Mercator said convincingly, 'You know, Ortelius, you could produce original maps and publish them, not just collect, colour and sell copies, even though you do those things profitably.'

'I'd have to think about that one,' Abraham said. Then he remembered that Mother had always told him to dream big dreams. Perhaps it could work out, as Homer once said, that a companion's words of persuasion are effective.

*

Frans Hogenberg was another of Abe's friends. 'Tell me about him,' I urged, for I liked him too despite his long nose and bushy eyebrows.

'He was raised near Antwerp at Mechelen in a family of artists and engravers. His father died when he was only two. He moved to Antwerp after his mother died. In Antwerp, being an engraver, he quickly made friends with a whole circle of engravers, printers, booksellers, humanists and other philosophers who were part of our bustling city. This was the beginning of my lifelong friendship with him.'

'He's one of your oldest and dearest friends, isn't he?' I said.

Abraham continued. 'He was in England with his brother Remigius for a while because of religious upheavals associated with the reign of terror that the Duke of Alva imposed in his quest to exterminate heresy in the Netherlands. There, Hogenberg spent time engraving portraits of members of the London court and etching views of the city of London. But eventually he came back to Antwerp to finish engraving maps for my *Theatrum*.'

'He surely travelled widely.'

'He did indeed. Later, Hogenberg moved to Cologne just over the border in Germany, a city safe from Spanish authority and political turmoil, where he set up a publishing house with a large staff. It was there that he engraved and published large maps, such as the Roman Empire based on my own design, and the Seventeen Provinces of the Netherlands. His engraving was praised as elegant. He also engraved thirty-two sheets of the History of Cupid and Psyche based on Raphael's designs.'

'That sounds like interesting work,' I said.

'He would agree with you there,' Abraham added.

'Some years afterwards, he visited Copenhagen and etched a family tree for the Danish governor. He also published two major print series at the time of the death of Frederick II of Denmark, in cooperation with Simon Novellanus. His output was prolific.'

3

I was always interested in the history of what was happening in the Netherlands, and kept up with political and religious goings on. Life marched unrelentingly onwards. Religious differences were multiplying, religious tension was mounting.

A new group, the Anabaptists, had grown out of Luther's teachings. They found a base in the Netherlands in 1534 but were never highly organised or in great numbers. Plus, they lacked strong leaders. They were disliked by both Catholics and Protestants. Many of them ended up on the scaffold.

In response to the rise in numbers of Protestants, the Catholic Church gathered in Trent for a council and redefined its own teachings to counter Protestant errors. It also gave more power to the Inquisition to stamp out Protestant heresy.

The Inquisition had arisen in Spain in the late 1400s to deal with the presence of Jews and Muslims in Catholic Spain. Earlier in our century, the Spanish kings acted against Protestants, using imprisonment, torture and execution to gain their ends. Abraham and I, like most other sensible people, did our best to keep our religious preferences to ourselves while outwardly declaring ourselves to be Catholic.

The Calvinists on the other hand were very successful in the Netherlands. In the 1560s, Calvinist leaders were engaged in outdoor preaching, for they weren't allowed to have their own churches.

*

Calvinist sympathisers had been forbidden to meet in cities, so they gathered in the countryside to hear what came to be known as hedgerow sermons. Abe and I went along once just for the experience. All sorts of people were there at those outlawed meetings: anyone, whether rich or poor, lay or religious, native born or foreigners, who wanted to hear about the new ideas. We also wanted to keep up with what was happening.

The Anabaptists, too, met in the open air. They practised adult baptism, just as John the Baptist had.

Peter Bruegel knew that his audience would recognise in any biblical scene that he painted some sort of symbolic comment on the times we lived in. He depicted a sermon of John the Baptist as a hedgerow sermon. And the message wasn't lost. The Baptist was indeed a suitable candidate to be giving the sermon, as he was eventually beheaded for preaching what was seen as heresy, just as some of the Calvinists and Anabaptists had been.

When Bruegel showed us his painting, he pointed to a corner. 'See the motley group that flocked out of Antwerp to hear what was being said. Peasants, craftsmen, members of the upper class, a pigtailed oriental, even nuns and monks. Some climbed a tree to get a better view, some hid behind trees so that they wouldn't be recognised.'

The small figure in the centre was the preacher John the Baptist.

'Maybe even I'm somewhere in the foreground!' said Bruegel.

*

It happened at the end of the long hot summer of 1566. It was one of the most atrocious things ever experienced. The Dutch called it the *Beeldenstorm*, the English called it the Iconoclasm.

It started with the hedgerow sermons. The perpetrators were mainly Calvinists. It swept through the Netherlands with great speed. Their grievances were many. They'd had enough. They had no churches to worship in and believed that Catholic worship of graven idols was against biblical values.

Other Protestants joined the revolt. Armed with sticks, axes and burning torches, they screamed as they smashed up churches, defaced carvings and statues, tore down and slashed paintings, and burnt books and vestments. It got out of hand as they assaulted priests, monks and nuns, even murdered a few, and intimidated and humiliated prominent Catholics. It was frightening and shocking. Everyone fled. Next day when we went to have a look at some of the damage, we found that all the churches looked as if evil itself had been at work for hundreds of years.

In our city alone on that ill-fated day, the cathedral, eight churches, twenty-five cloisters, ten hospitals and seven chapels were wrecked. What a stupendous and utterly wanton loss of some of the most wonderful architecture and art in the world.

Later, Abe wrote a letter about it to an out-of-town friend.

It looked like hell. There were more than ten thousand torches burning, and such a noise with the falling of statues and costly works. A large amount was stolen for while this was happening every whore and scoundrel took the opportunity to run through the church and carry away whatever they could find. The ruination was so great that a person couldn't even walk through the churches.

It really affected us all greatly at the time.

But one good thing to come out of it was that it did Martin de Vos a favour. It got him into public notice as an artist. He was still a developing painter at the time. Eventually, he had to come back from his studies in Italy to the Netherlands to earn a living, and in 1558 he joined the Guild of St Luke in Antwerp. That's when Abe first brought him home for a meal.

After the iconoclasm blew itself out and the Spanish again had the upper hand, de Vos told us that he was commissioned to paint pieces above the altars of some of the desecrated churches in Antwerp. It took him more than twenty years but he produced works that people greatly admired. I have seen some of his pieces in the cathedral at Antwerp: the *Marriage at Cana*, the *Nativity*, and *St Luke Painting the Virgin* that adorned the altar of the Guild of St Luke; and at St James church, the *Last Supper*. I found them to be beautiful.

4

You might ask what was happening in our family all this time.

Aunt Orillia had married Sir Jacob van Meteren in Antwerp in 1534. Emanuel was the eldest of their five children. After Father had passed away, Jacob was responsible for us children while we still lived with Mother. Even though Emanuel was considerably younger than Abraham, the two cousins grew up close to each other: the best of friends, almost like brothers.

In 1550, Jacob van Meteren had thought it unwise for his family to stay living in the Netherlands, so they sailed to London, where King Edward VI encouraged Protestant immigrants.

Uncle Jacob sent us a letter detailing the experience.

The ship was small and cramped, with not much air, and what there was, was cold and damp. The lack of space was especially trying for the children who found it difficult to do anything but retch all day. And the threat of pirates was very real. It was a rough passage over the Narrow Sea to England.

In London, we were able to join the Dutch Church, a church of Protestant refugees like ourselves. In fact, I quickly became one of its leaders before I fell ill.

He died within a year of their arrival.

I know that many Protestant refugees from northern Europe had taken their silk spinning and weaving skills with them to England and set up looms in their homes. There, they unravelled the gossamer thread from the cocoons and spun it into silk yarn as fine as a spider's web. Then they wove it into fabric lengths on their looms, and knitted stockings on special frames. Wealthy English ladies loved the brightness and lustre of silk material and their men were delighted not to have to import great rolls of the fabric any more.

Emanuel was fifteen when they left Antwerp. Later, when we saw him again, he told us that he had learnt the skills of a silk merchant. 'I began by hefting bolts of material around warehouses and recording and calculating figures and prices. After a few years, I was deemed old enough to travel to Europe, dealing in mulberry plants, silk cocoons and the silks themselves. I soon learnt to differentiate between the various grades of silks. Satins: glazed silks. Brocades: silks with raised patterns. Damasks: richly figured silks. Gauzes: very fine silks. Lustrings: glossy silks. And ribbons. Silk became a currency in itself, as good as gold and silver.'

In addition to his dealings in silk, Emanuel later became the person in the Dutch community in London who distributed letters on behalf of others. His network of contacts enabled him to send letters all over Europe, passing them from person to person until they reached their intended recipient. Sometimes, it would take months for a letter or parcel to arrive, easily held up by some forgetful person. Sometimes, they travelled by very circuitous routes as areas of flood, plague or war were avoided. Sometimes, they never arrived at all but found their home in the depths of the ocean as the ship carrying them floundered, or deep in some forest where rich merchants were likely to be attacked by robbers for their wealth. You had to be fairly lucky for your letter to reach its destination. Yet Abraham often had his maps sent to him by this method.

Emanuel's business dealings took him away from home a lot, visiting Dutch merchants both in England and Europe. He had a deep interest in Dutch history, an obsession even. So he would use opportunities provided by travel to visit scholars. He often boasted that one day he would write a definitive history of the wars in the Netherlands.

He came back to Antwerp from time to time, not only for business reasons but to catch up with us.

He visited us in 1562, the same year he married Marie, a twenty-two-year-old, who had already been imprisoned for her Calvinist faith. She had cunningly escaped through a hole in the wall of the prison. Emanuel admired her for her bravery as well as for her long golden curls. But she became ill in the following year and died. Not two years later, he married Hesta in a ceremony in Breda in the Netherlands where her family lived, but they considered it sensible to return London immediately afterwards. Together they had a large family of engaging children.

While Emanuel was in Antwerp in 1562 visiting us, he arranged for our sister, Elisabeth, to go back to London with him to live. He considered that it was now much safer there with Queen Elizabeth on the throne, free from the dangers of Antwerp with its constant suspicions, arrests and fighting over which religion was the one to follow.

Queen Elizabeth actively encouraged Protestants rather than oppressing them. So Emanuel and Elisabeth sailed across the Narrow Sea to London. Many Dutch families had left the area for London around this time so Elisabeth felt at home over there. Our families had joined a Protestant congregation of the Dutch Reformed Church.

Mother and Abe and I really missed Elisabeth when she left. So far away. Most of the map colouring fell to me after this.

It was in London that Elisabeth met a handsome silk and cloth merchant, Jacob Colius, who had lived there for about ten years. It was considered to be a good match. Both parties would benefit from an arranged marriage. It wasn't long before she was saying those familiar words, 'I, Elisabeth Ortels, take you, Jacob Colius, to be my lawful wedded husband.' The marriage ceremony was performed both in Antwerp and soon after in London. It wasn't practical – in fact, it was positively dangerous – for Jacob's older children from a previous marriage to come to Antwerp at this time.

It was good that we could be present at the wedding in Antwerp. Every girl likes her mother to help her dress for her special day. Elisabeth looked splendid in her rich burgundy gown of gold-patterned brocade with a silk underdress showing through a slit at the front. A square neckline was beaded with tiny pearls. On her head she wore a velvet French hood bordered in the same tiny pearls. Anne Boleyn, King Henry VIII's second wife, had made French hoods so popular. Around her neck lay a pearl-encrusted cross on a chain that Jacob had given her for the occasion. Abraham wasn't privy to all this women's business but he admired the finished product.

'My, how beautiful you look, my little one,' said Mother. 'Your father would have been so proud.'

'Lucky you,' I said, a little enviously.

The whole family enjoyed the celebrations. Abraham danced with me several times, delighting in the music and the rhythmic movement. He refrained from dancing with any of the other comely women at the feast.

He never really thought about getting married. He was mostly too busy to give but a passing glance to women, however good-looking, let alone love and cherish a wife. It wasn't that he was averse to having his own family. Our married friends mostly seemed happy enough. I thought that the problem was that Mother and I looked after him too well.

I took the opportunity to ask Elisabeth how she was finding life in London.

'My new surname, Colius, is a name that is easily Anglicised so we just became the Cools family and fitted in easily with English people despite their common suspicion of foreigners. The language was a problem for a while but we are getting our tongues around it now.'

At first, they lived in the mercantile district of London at Billingsgate near London Bridge.

Elisabeth came back again to Mother in Antwerp to have her first son, Jacob. What a dear little babe! Abraham held his new nephew in his arms and whispered endearments while gazing in wonderment at the sleeping little angel.

I'm not sure whether I would have liked to have a child or not. Anyway, the opportunity to marry has never presented itself to me, even though when I was younger I had a hankering for the baker's son. Looking after Mother and Abe was a full-time job, so I've never felt that I missed out on too much. However, I won't be called a spinster, even though I do spin threads for making clothing.

*

On one occasion while he was staying at Abraham's house in Antwerp, cousin Emanuel was arrested and imprisoned on charges of treason and heresy.

He told us the story. 'It was a Spaniard who arrested me; he came flanked by six halberdiers. They took my letters and keys, then went to your place and took all my writings and books. I was so scared, expecting torture and even death. I spent three days in a pitch-black prison. I prayed to God and thought about how to defend myself. Was it better to claim citizenship of Antwerp or of London, for in truth I was both.'

After four nights' imprisonment, Abraham, through some of his contacts, managed to obtain Emanuel's freedom. He was on the very next ship back to England.

Abraham too had been suspected of Protestant leanings but had managed to avoid trouble by keeping his opinions to himself and slipping across the Narrow Sea to stay with family in London during the fiercest years of political storms.

'Dear Emanuel,' he wrote, 'We live in a very disordered time, which we have little hope of seeing improved. Antwerp will soon be entirely prostrate, being threatened with so many illnesses: the Catholic evil, the Calvinist rebels' revolutionary fever, and the Protestant dysentery mixed with other vexations of black horsemen and soldiers.'

The black-coated soldiers and their horses referred to the Spanish Duke of Alva and his troops.

5

In my experience, politics never remain constant, that's for certain.

After Charles V's abdication in 1556, the Seventeen Provinces of the Netherlands passed to his son, Philip II, the new king of Spain. Three years later, Philip II appointed his half-sister, Margaret of Parma, regent in the Netherlands while he left to live in Spain. She resigned in 1567. Philip also invited the Jesuits to work in the Netherlands hoping that they would strengthen Catholicism.

We Antwerpians had thought things with regard to the Spanish and the Inquisition were bad before 1567. We were wrong. They got much worse when Philip II sent Fernando Alvarez de Toledo, known as the Duke of Alva, with ten thousand troops to put down Protestant heresy in our country once and for all, and to restore order.

Alva built a star-shaped fortress in the defensive walls of Antwerp on the southern side of the city and garrisoned his troops within. Its presence was a constant reminder to us that these times were dangerous.

*

Peter Bruegel was living in Brussels when the Duke of Alva marched his army into Antwerp in August 1567. The commander's orders were to forcibly convert Protestant heretics.

'I would rather sacrifice the lives of a hundred thousand people than let up in my persecution of heretics,' Alva was once heard to exclaim.

'What a pompous bastard!' was Bruegel's response to that. He had a way with words.

There were religious wars going on in France at this time too, so that Alva was unable to take the direct route from Spain to the Netherlands. He was forced to sail to Italy and then march over the Alps and through Germany to the Low Countries.

Later, when Bruegel was visiting us again, he told us how Alva had inspired his painting the *Conversion of St Paul*. 'What Biblical image could I paint to reflect these goings on?' he had wondered. 'How about the moment of conversion of St Paul on the road to Damascus? Paul, the arrogant Jew, was out to persecute Christians back in those times. If I were to depict Paul flung onto the ground in his moment of conversion in a craggy alpine setting in the midst of a Spanish army, would that get the message across? I think so.'

So right in the middle of the painting, high up on a mountain track is the rear view of a large horseman wearing black clothes and riding a white stallion. The backside of Alva and his horse loomed much larger than Paul himself.

'I think that did it!' Bruegel exclaimed.

*

The measures that Philip, through the Duke of Alva, employed against Dutch Protestants were often despotic and unjust. Eventually, the people rose in rebellion, not only because of religious issues but also because Philip taxed us to the hilt to support his armies and cut back people's rights and freedoms.

One of the Duke of Alva's first actions in the Netherlands was to set up the Council of Troubles, which conducted a fierce campaign against heresy. We called it the Council of Blood. Some of the nobility and state leaders were executed, even though they vowed they were Catholics. Nine thousand were accused, more than a thousand executed, many fled the country for fear of their lives. Our Prince William of Orange fled from the south to the north of the Netherlands and took up his cause against the Spanish in earnest.

Preparations were at once made to gather troops and wage war against Philip's forces in the Netherlands. Then followed the long, ghastly struggle between the armies raised by William of Orange and those of Alva and his successors.

William of Orange, or William the Silent as he was sometimes known, embraced the Calvinist faith and the leadership of the Dutch. It was in the north of the Seventeen Provinces that he was most successful in gaining a following. He set out to free the Calvinist Dutch from the Catholic Spaniards, and Antwerp was right in the middle of the resulting turmoil.

What was to become known as the Dutch revolt began at this time and went on for years. In fact, it was still going on when Abraham died.

It wasn't a continuous war with constant fighting but rather a disconnected series of battles, massacres and sieges. A long drawn-out process of hostility not only between the Netherlands and the Spanish, between Protestants and Catholics, but also between the north and south of the Netherlands. The result was anarchy. Terrifyingly dangerous times to be living in.

*

Another of Bruegel's paintings, this time the *Massacre of the Innocents*, was supposedly about the consequences of Herod's decree at the time Christ was born: a decree that all children under two years of age should be slaughtered so that Herod's kingship would be assured from this potential usurper.

Or was it? Looking closely at the painting it can be seen that it was set in a snowbound Dutch village where the bitter northern cold cut as cruelly as the swords of the soldiers of the attacking foreign troops.

The Duke of Alva, notorious for his ruthlessness, was a man who instilled terror wherever he went. He marched into towns and villages with his soldiers armed with their long pikes and spears. Thousands of innocents were killed simply for believing in a different way. It's no wonder that we Netherlanders rose up in revolt against him.

Abraham's comment was, 'It is patently clear that the man in the painting's middle foreground mounted on a white horse and dressed in black is Alva.'

6

Nevertheless, daily life had to go on. As long as we were careful about what we said and who we said it to, we mostly managed to keep out of trouble and continue living fairly normal lives in times when the troubles didn't directly impinge on Antwerp.

The humanist circle that Abraham belonged to met at either our house or Plantin's. When Plantin first settled in Antwerp, he got to know many business associates and their friends with a similar outlook on life. It was when Father Arias Montanus came to Antwerp from Spain to publish his polyglot Bible that he introduced Plantin to humanist ideas, and a group of like-minded people began to get together regularly.

There were about twenty of them, more or less, at any particular time, as people came and went. As many came along as could, but it was always enough for a lively and long discussion which I could overhear if I procrastinated while serving food and drink to the group. This nucleus of people who became close friends centred on Plantin. He led the way and often did the gathering, providing the chairs and the beer. Over the years all sorts of people came along: there were engravers, painters, printers, merchants, numismatists and others too. All these people saw themselves, their art and their work as much wider than their occupations suggested. They were all thinkers and scholars. Some lived in other parts of the country, so they came along when they were in Antwerp for business or kept up a correspondence which was read at the gatherings.

Although Antwerp's humanists enjoyed a reputation among European scholars, they only shared their ideas among themselves, not just with anybody. It was safer that way.

Every one of these people studied the ancient classics and knew Latin. Some who missed out on Latin in their childhood education learnt the language on their own initiative so that they could better appreciate the old writings. And Plantin made sure that he printed plenty of Latin literature both old and new. That certainly sealed his place in the circle.

It took me some time to begin to understand the essence of humanism. Abraham believed it was impossible to capture it in a few words. It was something that gave meaning to their whole lives. They lived and breathed it every moment of the waking day and dreamt about it at night.

An important part of it was a constant effort to understand the cultures of the ancient Greeks and Romans. Humanists recognised that the greatness of those cultures was lost when barbarians took over the world. They discovered again ancient literature, art, architecture, science – every branch of learning. And then attempted to understand it all in the light of our own day and age.

Abraham told me that the Italians had first introduced the movement into Europe in the fourteenth century when fleeing Ottomans brought ancient manuscripts to Florence: manuscripts that Europe had not had access to since before the time of the barbarians, manuscripts that opened people's eyes again to what life could be.

'The ancient languages of Latin and Greek underpinned humanism,' he said. 'Not just any old dog-Latin like that taught in schools, but the clear and classical elegance of the ancient tongue. To be able to communicate and persuade in elegant Latin, using Cicero as a model, was a must for a humanist.'

Sometimes, we women got together and swapped understandings of our men's ideas about life. Gradually we figured most of it out.

As I came to understand it, humanism is basically a philosophy of life that values what it is to be fully human as opposed to attributing all aspects of life to the will of God. It affirms people's ability and responsibility to lead ethical lives, lives of personal fulfilment, lives that aspired to a greater good. Perhaps it would become clearer to know a little of what people in Abraham's humanist circle thought and believed.

*

Plantin often spoke of his ideas when at our place. He believed that individual human fulfilment came from honest employment, employment that was of some benefit to society. He said that in his profession as a printer and publisher, he aimed to produce useful works, especially those of scientific value and artistic worth. He concentrated on the simplest as well as the greatest of his publications. He chose carefully the subjects to be published and adorned his books in good taste. Above all, he tried to produce a huge number and variety of books for people to read. He had translations made from Latin into Dutch and French so ordinary people could read them. And he kept good relations with his assistants and provided them with conditions to make their job more enjoyable. His object in all this was not simply to make money. No, rather, for him, as for Abraham, it was a way of life that was deeply human and satisfying.

Plantin's motto was *Labore et constantia*. By hard work and tenacity, or With toil and perseverance. One of his trademarks showed a hand reaching out of the clouds holding a compass. One point was fixed, for constancy. The other marked a circle, for labour. Other elements of the trademark, the elaborate borders of foliage and figures, were changed frequently. He hung it above the door of his workshop and put it on the back page of most of the books that he printed.

*

Abraham met with Peter Bruegel fairly regularly in their circle of friends. Lutherans and Calvinists both, they held conversations about religious issues of the country, particularly the conflicts between Catholics and Protestants: Bruegel had always been fascinated by the struggle between being an individual and being a Christian; the struggle was a constant one. This is what lay behind his painting *Battle Between Carnival and Lent.*

The painting shows a mock battle between Carnival and Lent. Carnival is the period immediately before the start of Lent when people fully indulged, before the austerity of Lenten fasting. A grossly fat and brightly dressed man sitting atop a beer barrel is Carnival, ready to joust with Lent, a scrawny creature on the other side of the painting, clad in mourning clothes and sitting on an uncomfortable prayer stool. Carnival wields a cooking spit topped with a pig's head while Lent waves a baker's paddle holding two small fish. On one side of the painting, men engage in brawls in front of an inn and beggars are ignored. In contrast, the other side is filled with pious people doing good works. Black-robed worshippers are coming out of an austere church, a fishmonger plies his wares beside a well and kindly citizens dispense alms. The whole painting can be seen as a battle between good and piety on the one hand, and evil and self-indulgence on the other.

Both sides represented excesses of our day. Bruegel's friends condemned the hypocrisy that went on between Protestants and Catholics, not only at the beginning of Lent but at all times. They disapproved of a life that results from both excessive fasting and excessive feasting. In the painting the figures who come into the square from the church door are emaciated with black cloaks. The Carnival group suffered from their greed. Neither overindulgence nor fasting brings contentment. But in the centre of the picture, a middle road between both excesses is represented by a man in a broad-brimmed hat and a woman in a plain black dress who travel through the scene calmly amid life's disorder. And surely, I thought, this image applies not only to Lent but to the rest of the year too.

Bruegel and Abraham refrained from taking sides in any of this; they found fault with the extremes of both. It was more diplomatic that way in the current climate of the times.

*

Dirck Coornhert was another who had a great interest in humanism, being a theologian and a philosopher of sorts. He even wrote a book about it, in Dutch so that many more people could read and understand and perhaps follow humanist ideas.

Everyone knew of Coornhert and had heard about what he'd done and what he believes. His full name was Dirck Volckertszoon Coornhert; his second name just meant that he was the son of Volckerts. He was known as an engraver, a translator, politician, lawyer, poet and playwright, philosopher and theologian, spiritualist and controversialist. In short, a man of many parts. And very proficient.

And what did Abraham know of Dirck Coornhert? He knew him as a fellow humanist, but Abraham didn't really like him. Something about Coornhert irked him.

Coornhert's steady gaze and kindly face revealed what a friendly fellow he could be if it suited him, but he always stood his ground for what he knew was right.

He started out in Antwerp as an engraver. He shared an interest in anything classical and belonged to the same circle of friends who discussed deeply philosophical ideas. Coornhert went to gatherings whenever he was in Antwerp, and between times he wrote letters.

'I bet,' he was heard to say to Abraham, 'that controversialist was the title from my skills that you first noticed. I've been involved in arguments with Calvinists practically since Calvin first appeared on our scene. I got into public debates whenever and wherever I could get a hearing.' He was not afraid to speak his mind.

Calvin always advocated that faith requires a church, whereas Coornhert considered that a person could be a good believer without a church. Abraham agreed with that. They both believed that the basis of a Christian life was to love God and one's neighbour, and that ceremonies and rites were human in origin, rather than based on the Bible.

'Have you guessed that both Coornhert and I are still Catholics at heart even though the outward trappings of organised religion mean very little to us?' Abraham asked me.

Coornhert didn't just criticise the system, he worked within it. He was for some time secretary to the city and its burgomeister. He wrote pamphlets and news-sheets for Prince William of Orange in the latter's struggle against Spanish rule. William liked his direct and plain-speaking style.

Abraham said that Coornhert learnt Latin at a later age than most in order to read the classics. And then, so that everyone could read the classics, he translated Cicero, Seneca and Homer into Dutch. He was an intelligent man and had a natural ability to write so that the not-so-learned could understand him. He tried to use his talents to help wherever he could: a modern-day good Samaritan.

It was Coornhert's determination to be controversial that irked Abraham, who preferred to be passive in the public arena.

*

Bruegel once said, 'I don't know why painters keep producing portraits of noble gentlemen and their women, grandiose as they are, and vignettes of religious women and men, uplifting as they are, when there is a whole seething mass of beautiful humanity out there just waiting to be transformed onto canvas. Peasants, beggars and cripples going about their work, play and seduction. What better way to acknowledge their equality as humans with the high and mighty than to have paintings of them hanging for all to see and admire? What's more, such paintings give wealthier people the opportunity to see how others live out their humble lives.'

Bruegel deemed that it wasn't enough just to view peasants in their own environment, but that one should also experience life as they do. City dwellers lived a relatively privileged life and didn't know what it's like on the other side. So he and a friend went out into the countryside, dressed suitably, pretending to be peasants and joining in their celebrations, walking in their shoes as it were, and sketched images of peasant life.

'I can just imagine him skipping around and laughing and clapping with the rustics,' said Abraham, grinning.

Bruegel painted a series of six paintings, one for each season, that showed ordinary people going about their ordinary work. He set them in elegant landscapes; that was another of his passions, painting landscapes.

'Look at *Corn Harvesters*,' he pointed out. 'It's summertime. Some are cutting the shoulder-high grain, some are gathering it into piles, and others are stacking the piles pyramid-fashion to make stooks so that it can dry out. Then there are workers who are taking a break to eat, sitting beneath a tree, sprawled out in all sorts of ungainly poses and in all sorts of garish clothes. You may or may not notice that the painting illustrates more than the work that marks the time of the year. Important also is the bright yellow atmosphere marking a successful harvest and the hope and joy that it brings. Surely a few birds trilled in the trees.'

'And what about this painting set in the depths of winter?' I asked.

'Well, it has a similar message,' Bruegel replied. '*Hunters in the Snow* shows a village landscape in winter with a group of hunters returning, head down, empty-handed and dejected from the hunt, along with their equally depressed-looking dogs. Skaters and curlers are on the ice, hungry black crows perch in bare trees on the lookout for some morsel of food. And there in the background lie pristine icy mountains towards which the hunters are, at least metaphorically, heading. One has to have a vision after all, no matter how helpless one feels about the changeability of life and unsuccessful hunts.'

I noticed how happy the corn harvesters looked producing their crops in honest employment so that all could eat. And weren't the hunters just as industrious even though their landscape was bleak at the moment of the painting? Abraham, along with Bruegel and Plantin and all the others, thought that a good measure of fulfilment came from honest work that had some benefit to society.

Bruegel valued artistic creativity and imagination, and 'recognised the transformative power of paintings', as the humanists would say.

*

Early in autumn in 1569, when the biting winter winds began to howl around his house, Peter Bruegel was confined to his bed with some unknown sickness that anyone could predict was going to be fatal. He didn't know what ailment he had contracted but it was surely taking its toll. He was just fading away. He looked like a bag of bones and hurt like hell.

Abraham went to visit him.

Bruegel told him that there was so much more that he wanted to paint, so much more to learn about life. 'But I no longer have the energy,' he said. 'It's all I can do to raise my head from the pillow.'

As he lay there helplessly, he confided to Abraham his worries about what would happen to his wife and two little sons. He hoped that Mayken would marry again. He had told Mayken to burn the unsold paintings and drawings in the studio. 'Some of them may be seen as traitorous,' he said. 'They could get you into trouble with the Inquisition.'

And he worried about his children. His son, Peter, was just beginning to make colourful splashes with a paintbrush on any surface that he deemed suitable and Jan hadn't even had his first birthday yet. Bruegel hoped that his mother-in-law would teach them to paint, for she was a fine artist herself.

All of this Abraham shared with me when he got home again. He summed up Bruegel's life: a life that had been enriched by painting, allegorising, seeking beauty and speaking politically through the medium of art.

'But his pain was unbearable,' he said.

*

'Let's go down to the river and do a bit of fishing,' I said. 'Some fresh air might do you some good.'

'Do we have to?' was the reply.

'It's time you put aside your grieving for Peter, got away from your usual pursuits and did something a bit more relaxing and enjoyable.

65

And we could do with a change of diet. A nice fresh fish would be just the thing.'

'I admit that I could do with a break,' he said, 'but don't go thinking that I don't enjoy everything I do. There may be some stress sometimes but on the whole, I delight in my work.'

Abe put on his coat and hat while I gathered the pole and line along with some nets. It wasn't very far to our favourite rock. A brisk breeze was blowing across the river creating small choppy waves and sending salty aromas our way. I drew my shawl tighter.

Abe arranged his rug around his shoulders and settled down with a resigned sigh. He soon had his pole dangling in the water with a lump of bread on the hook at the bottom of the line. Seagulls surrounded us squawking for a morsel.

'Got one!' he said excitedly, and nearly fell into the river as he bent to its sudden tug.

'Quick, pull it in,' I urged him.

'Yes, yes, I know.' But he wasn't quick enough and it got away.

I watched the water very intently with my net at the ready should another fish come my way.

Eventually, Abe caught a nice fat perch. 'This is not worth keeping,' he said. 'It's a lousy fish to eat.' He threw it back into the water.

As always, Abe quickly got bored waiting for a fish to nibble at his bait. 'Did I happen to tell you…' He soon launched into another tale of his exploits.

While I didn't really want to hear another story, it gave him pleasure in the telling, so I banished my thoughts of a tasty pike for dinner and listened with half an ear.

*

One of the discussions that often engaged their humanist circle and was later related to me was about finding a blend of Christianity and classical thought that would act as a guide to conduct in life.

Abraham was a bit obsessed with Cicero and often quoted bits and pieces from his writings. One of his favourite quotes, and one that he certainly embraced was, 'Be content with what you have; that is the greatest and truest of riches.' Another that Abe strived to live by, but not always successfully, was, 'Live as the brave do: if fortune is adverse, face its blows with brave hearts.' I do believe that Abe was brave, at least in his heart, though not always in action.

Abraham agreed with Bruegel, who had recognised that life can be nasty and short, and nature can be cruel and indifferent to human needs. But the search for meaning through everyday struggles is a never-ending quest.

Abraham said that he was attracted to membership in the Family of Love that Plantin often talked about. 'They believe that they are above the often-empty religious practices of both Protestants and Catholics,' he said. 'They hold fast to an inward spirituality that has at its heart a personal knowledge of God.'

That would just about sum up what I know of my brother's inner life, regardless of the Family of Love.

I guess that when it came to the point, it would have been difficult to discover what each person's 'religion' was. Allegiance often switched rapidly according to the situations of danger that people found themselves in. I know all in the humanist circle abhorred the persecution and wars that arose from the Spanish insistence that not to be Catholic was heretical, with consequences. Not only Catholics but Lutherans and Calvinists had their share of persecution in different ways. And they all vehemently believed that peace was the only way forward.

I certainly whole-heartedly agree with all that. If there were such a thing as a pacifist, Abe would be one.

*

Abraham came to belong to the Family of Love. So did Plantin, Coornhert and Father Arias Montanus, the Catholic monk. And in England, so did Emanuel van Meteren and John Dee. Even Queen Elizabeth was an admirer. So it was a widespread and readily accepted way of life.

In its essence, the Family of Love was a secret movement. Members kept themselves to themselves without telling the world what they believed. The movement took in members of various religions, but whatever branch they belonged to wasn't the point. It was the Familist ideals that they lived by.

Abraham told me about the history of the movement. 'It was Hendrik Niclaes, a Dutch cloth merchant, who began it. He believed that God had told him in a revelation that Christians should rely on an inner light and God's love rather than on rites and sacraments. He stressed peace and unity above denominational loyalty. He encouraged an inner spirituality searching for a direct relationship with God – a mystical union with God, as some people called it.'

The human heart is a symbol of this spirituality: the heart, the source of divine enlightenment and love. Abraham once even made a map based on a heart-shaped projection.

I am aware that Familists strive for religious tolerance in a world divided by religious wars. They believe that the different faiths are substantially the same, including those of the Jews and the Muslims. And that there can be a common inner spirituality and quest for goodness. For the most part, they read the Bible allegorically rather than literally, and deny that such places as heaven and hell exist. They scorn the superstitious healing powers of relics.

'But,' Abe often said, 'none of this is in isolation from the broader philosophies that we discuss in our humanist circle. Life is an integrated thing, not something divided into categories. As Aristotle once said, "The whole is greater than the sum of its parts."'

*

Another friend of Abraham's – he had lots of them – was Joris Hoefnagel, who too was a humanist and belonged to the circle. He was small and lean, his curly hair matched his meticulously pointed beard and moustache. A bit like a forest elf. While never embracing the latest fashion, his appearance was always very dapper.

Abraham had heard that Joris's father wanted him to go into his diamond business with him, but then realised the futility of his own hopes when all Joris wanted to do was paint and engrave. However, later on and out of necessity, Joris did combine dealing in jewels with his art.

Abraham admired his work. 'He is a self-taught artist,' he said. 'He dabbled in many different kinds of painting and drawing, always with an eye for minutiae that included, where appropriate, fine details of petals of flowers, scales of fish and feathers of birds. He is known for his delicate miniature and illuminative work, especially in books containing church services. He paints allegories of all the seasons. He writes Latin poetry, has learnt several languages and plays a variety of musical instruments. A versatile artist but also a dreamer, he always sees his dreams to fruition.'

A bit like you, Abe, I thought.

Abraham continued, 'When Hoefnagel was younger, he travelled through France, Spain, Italy and England. The journeys were funded by his father's diamonds. Everywhere he went, he sketched landscapes, vistas of cities and places of interest.'

We had one of Hoefnagel's paintings, *Hermathena*, hanging in the front room of our house. And later, Hoefnagel sketched an entry for Abraham's *Album Amicorum*, his book of friends.

7

Perhaps one of Abraham's dearest friends was Mercator. He was certainly a member of the humanist circle and encouraged Abraham in his map making.

Abraham talked about him and his work a lot. 'One of the ways that humanism spread throughout northern Europe was through the universities,' he said. 'Not through their formal curriculum but by itinerant scholars who gave talks and held discussions in campus quadrangles. Students travelled from place to place to hear lecturers at different universities. I guess it was one of those enthusiastic scholars who changed Mercator's course in life from what he had set out on and turned his interest to geography. Certainly he spent hours and hours studying Ptolemy's *Geographica*, and writing an updated version of it. A key part of Ptolemy's work was instructions on how to draw maps. He had plotted locational coordinates of thousands of places.'

Abe certainly knew a lot about a lot of ancient experts.

He went on to explain that one of Mercator's main interests in cartography was the development of a new map projection. 'It took much time and mathematical skill to work it out,' he said. 'The projection was a cylindrical one. It was like this: if a piece of paper was wrapped into a cylindrical shape around the globe, then a light at the centre of the globe would project onto the paper the lines of latitude and longitude that would then appear as straight lines at right angles to each other. He wasn't the first to invent such a projection, but he refined it so that compass bearings could be plotted in straight lines on navigational charts. So he provided seamen with a partial solution to the old problem of navigation at sea.'

'I'm not sure that I understand all that,' was my response.

So he further explained that by applying this projection, shapes of continents were not always true: the further from the equator, the greater the distortion. This made shapes and distances reasonably accurate to about 60° of latitude north and south: the area in which lay most of the known world.

Frankly, I suspect that Abraham didn't really understand mathematics to such a great a depth either, but he was very good at selecting only the best maps and then editing, updating and accurately presenting them. He used the data of explorers, geographers and previous cartographers as far back as Ptolemy and always made sure to get permission to revise maps of living cartographers. His maps were a great improvement on previous maps of the regions. And he was a much better artist than Mercator could ever be, so Abe's maps had a mass appeal that initially Mercator's didn't.

*

Until the mid-1560s, Abraham had spent a lot of time travelling and looking for maps to take back to Antwerp and colour before selling them on again for a higher price.

One day, Abe confided in me. 'While away on that trip through Trier in 1560, Mercator argued that I had a lot more in me than was needed for colouring and dealing in maps, so he encouraged me to become a maker of maps, to draw them myself.' This was a new venture.

'I wondered whether I could do it. What if it didn't work out? I could spend a lot of time and end up with an unsatisfactory result. And what if I failed to gain the necessary privilege, or permission to publish? All that work would be in vain.'

Although I intuitively knew that Abraham could do it, he lacked a certain amount of confidence in himself.

I watched as Abe first used someone else's maps as a basis and brought them up to date by correcting any mistakes and adding new information that he had gleaned from talking to geographers, mapmakers and sea captains. Then he added his own embellishments, often using cartouches from the collection of others. It wasn't long before he left me to add whatever extras he wanted on his maps. He still had to have his maps re-engraved from the outset.

It was in 1564 that Abraham published his own first map. He started out on a large scale, producing an eight-sheet heart-shaped map of the world, a *mappemonde* he called it, surrounded by a variety of windheads. It was an ambitious project, so large it could only hang on a wall.

'The cordiform projection's a bit of a novelty,' was Mercator's response when he first saw the map, 'but Ptolemy made cordiform maps. He's a good model to follow for your first map.'

Expanding on his choice of projection, Abraham replied, 'There is also something in it of the Family of Love. We use the heart as a symbol, just as the Jesuits did. You know, the heart is where the loving is, and the inner battle between good and evil goes on.'

*

In the following year, Abraham produced a two-sheet map of Egypt that he dedicated to Scipio Fabio, the Italian humanist and medical doctor from Bologna. I looked on as he put it together. As the interior of Egypt away from the Nile River has hardly been explored, he left bare gaps in the middle of the map. Abraham asked me to fill them with mountains, date palms and camels.

Abe was quickly caught up with making his own maps. Next, he made an eight-sheet map of Asia that was based on a map by the Italian, Giacomo Gastaldi, who in turn had based his map on that of an Arab geographer of the early fourteenth century known as Albufeda. Abraham included some images that Marco Polo had drawn, and the locations of some interior Asian areas, such as Tibet and Tangut, whose people had fought the Mongolians in previous centuries. And, to fill up the empty space, I drew a pair of lions in the centre of China. Empty spaces were always a challenge. Near New Guinea, I placed an especially handsome bird of paradise with a mass of showy feathers.

Then he made a plan of the archeological site of Arx Britannica, the ruins of a Roman frontier fort. It lay just off the coast of the Netherlands and was visible when low tide coincided with the full moon. The plan was inserted into a topographical view of the surrounding landscape. He included some texts from Tacitus's *Germania*, some drawings of carvings and several inscriptions in marble that were found there.

In his research, he found that Arx Britannica had been used by the Roman army as a storehouse for weapons and a base for excursions to Britain from the mouth of the Rhine. Abraham greatly enjoyed this project as it brought to life an aspect of an ancient culture that had long gone.

Early in 1570, he produced a six-sheet wall map of Spain. The Spaniard, Carol Clusius, gave him a lot of information that was incorporated into this map. Clusius was always travelling for his studies of plants and gardens. Abraham noted that the ancient Strabo said that the shape of Spain, surrounded by sea on three sides, looked like an ox-hide spread out on the ground.

Wall maps were mounted on linen, pasted on with glue made of flour and boiling water. That was another of my jobs. The maps usually had distinctive borders so that the individual pieces could be lined up accurately when assembled to wall size, where they hung from a pole or on a roller.

It was Mercator who gave my brother the idea of assembling maps of all the parts of the world in one accessible place. How useful that would be to explorers, seafarers and merchants, and how convenient to have all their maps in one volume. Abraham had kept the idea in the back of his mind for many years.

He confessed that Mercator was also determined to put together such a mapbook too. However, Mercaor thought it might be years before he'd get around to it, so busy did other people keep him. Inspired by the mythical person of Atlas, condemned to carry the world on his shoulders, Mercator said that he planned to call his mapbook an atlas.

*

While the ambitious Gerard de Jode wasn't exactly a close friend of Abraham, they tolerated each other. They had to, to get things done. Abraham had asked him to print his huge map of the world, made in eight sheets to be joined together and attached to a wall. De Jode did so. It proved to be a turning point in Abraham's career and made his business ever more lucrative.

Nearly twenty years older than Abraham, de Jode was somewhat put out by my brother's success. Abraham overheard him muttering, 'How could any cartographer worth his salt ever compete with Abraham Ortelius?' His dour face, etched with a self-imposed authority, was twisted with dislike. Abraham ignored him.

'Tell me more about this man,' I asked. 'What's his background?'

'De Jode came to Antwerp from Nijmegen in the northern Netherlands in 1547 and was admitted to the Guild of St Luke. Two years later, he became a citizen of Antwerp and obtained a licence to publish. Soon, he was running a print shop with five engravers and dealing regularly with Plantin. He visited the Frankfurt Book Fair a couple of times too. I remembered seeing him there once or twice.'

I had heard that de Jode was a cartographer, an engraver, and a printer and publisher of mainly maps. Besides maps, he engraved and published a few paintings, mostly compositions by others, including Martin de Vos and Michelangelo. Although a late starter, he was well considered in Antwerp and beyond as an accomplished cartographer and printer. Abraham saw him as serious competition.

Later, de Jode published maps of the most important countries in quick succession. Some of these he himself drafted and engraved, but most of them were engraved by others.

Word had got out that for some time Abraham was collecting maps for a compendium. De Jode was thinking about doing the same. He was still thinking about it while my brother got on with it.

8

Abraham liked to visit Gillis Hooftman's office and warehouses, as Gillis had a great collection of maps. He was a wealthy merchant of Antwerp, a very wealthy merchant; in fact, he was an extremely influential man. And he was quick to let people know about it.

'It wasn't always so,' said Abraham. 'Born in Germany, he came to Antwerp in 1547. He built up his business empire by hard work and a good deal of cunning, and by making the most of opportunities that came his way. With its banks and Exchange, Antwerp was a very advantageous place to live for an up-and-coming businessman. Ships brought spices from the Indies, silver from South America and cloth from England. Hooftman imported luxury goods like furs and caviar in return for wine and precious metals. He exported tons of timber. He even had offices in London. He owned more than a hundred ships, which sailed to the Baltic as well as north African ports. He pioneered Dutch trade way up north on the White Sea and had connections at the English court of Queen Elizabeth. He was also an expert in seamanship and navigation.'

I was with Abe at his office one day when I heard Hooftman moaning. 'So I need maps of distant countries as new places are discovered,' he said, 'and new trading develops. Lots of maps, maps for every part of the world. I've got a great many, so many that I don't know where to put them all.'

I could see that he had a huge up-to-date map of the world on his wall and one of Europe on which he placed pins to show where he traded. He said he obtained new maps every few years to keep up with the latest discoveries. He found maps irresistible.

He said, 'I've backed painters, scientists and artisans, including the painter Martin de Vos, as well as you, Ortelius. You are the expert at obtaining really up-to-date maps for me.'

Hooftman owned several places in Antwerp. He lived in a big house, the Groote Gans, the Great Goose, next to his extensive warehouses. Martin de Vos had decorated the interior of Hooftman's house with fancy murals. 'Opulence itself,' was Hooftman's summary.

'By the way, Ann,' Hooftman asked while I was there. 'Did you see the portrait that Martin de Vos painted of me with my ruddy nose and flowing beard, along with my good wife Margaretha? Handsome, isn't it?'

Abraham continued with his appraisal of Hooftman's life. 'He provided money, arms and provisions for Prince William of Orange and the revolutionaries who sided with the Protestant cause in their rebellion against Spain. Just after the *Beeldenstorm*, his name had appeared on a list prepared by the Inquisition of rich Calvinists to be persecuted. Good thing he avoided that one!' He laughed.

*

But Gillis Hooftman's story of his love affair with his maps didn't end there.

One day, he said to Abraham, 'This office is a pigsty. All these maps strewn about: huge maps that take up most of a wall, small maps with tiny writing that would bedevil any short-sighted fellow, rolled-up maps that stick out at all angles, flat maps in great piles, and folded maps that need unfolding every time I need to consult them. How could I ever find the one I wanted at the moment I need it?'

Abraham had often wondered that too. Hooftman had bought just about every map and chart that he'd been able to lay his hands on. He'd financed some of Abraham's map-finding trips abroad. Abraham called him his patron, and that he was, but he'd certainly made a profit from Abraham's endeavours.

'It's not that I'm belittling maps at all. Where would I be without them?' he said. 'My mercantile network has been built on maps. My ships would never find their way to foreign ports without them.'

He'd been able to use maps to plot those locations in which wars were raging so as to avoid them, to work out the shortest and safest ways to transport merchandise overland and to figure out what freight rates to charge. Freight rates were very important to a merchant.

Hooftman studied the seas, the tides and the winds trying to figure out the best routes for his ships and the best times to send them on their way to foreign ports.

'But do you think I can keep my maps under control?' he grumbled. 'I was complaining to my assistant the other day when he came up with a new idea. Why don't I get you, Ortelius, to put some of my smaller maps into a book, then they would all be in the one place.'

So Abraham did just that. He put together thirty-eight maps of Europe, Asia, Africa, Tartary and Egypt. They were all different sizes and straggling at the edges, but they were all in one book so that Hooftman could take them anywhere with him.

Soon after that, Hooftman looked intently at Abraham with his beady eyes and said, 'Now we should get you to work on a mapbook that has maps all the one size. That would really be something!'

*

Gillis Coppens van Diest was getting old. His hair was already snowy white and his brow wrinkled. He had just celebrated his seventy-third birthday. However, he was still an excellent printer and publisher.

'In fact,' Abraham reported, 'until Plantin arrived in Antwerp, he was the biggest of them all. He was famous for printing massive works with engraved illustrations and decorative initials. He often printed texts for other publishers as well as for authors. I know you like to hear all about my associates,' said Abe, 'so here's another story for you. There was a time when the Spanish Inquisition accused van Diest of printing suspect authors and circulating Protestant pamphlets. He wasn't going to admit his guilt, especially as recently a colleague had been beheaded for the same activity. Earlier, the king's regent had instructed her men to find who was responsible for a heretical book and to inquire among the printers as to who used the particular typeface. All the Antwerp printers said that they knew nothing about it. On another occasion, the printer of a secret pamphlet needed to be identified. Van Diest had printed this text too, but he declared that everyone used that typeface. One of his colleagues indicated that he had used the same typeface, but the suspicious text was in Dutch whereas he usually used Latin. They had to back each other up or they'd all be in the fire, so to speak.'

It was because of his vast experience in printing and publishing that Abraham gave van Diest the honour of issuing the first edition of his mapbook, *Theatrum orbis terrarum*.

Part Two

1570

Theatrum Orbis Terrarum

9

At last it was finished! It took hours of work by many people over a couple of years. But on 20 May 1570, it was published. Abraham's *Theatrum orbis terrarum*, his pride and joy.

Mercator sent him a letter saying how pleased he was with the end result of the *Theatrum* that Abraham had laboured long over. Mercator had encouraged him and allowed him to use his best maps. And Abraham was so pleased with this response that he included the letter in the 1573 and subsequent editions of the *Theatrum*.

A thousand congratulations to you, Abraham Ortelius, my good friend, on the production of your *Theatrum*. From now on your reputation as a cartographer will never be in doubt; you will receive the highest accolades. You truly deserve all the honours and wealth that will come to you from this publication.

Well done too, Ortelius, to have dedicated the *Theatrum* to King Philip II. That is sure to give you added prestige.

Not only the rich and the learned, but ordinary people will read your *Theatrum* with pleasure, enjoying the visual beauty of the world and the written accompaniments that are far more than descriptions for travellers. Your mapbook will become the accepted vision of the world. You wrote in your introduction that geography is the eye of history. So much will be learned about the past as well as the present, and we will be looking forward to future discoveries and new editions that will reflect new information as it comes to hand.

You will be remembered for your ability to gather an immense body of existing geographic knowledge and publish it in the consistent and high-quality form of the mapbook. The essence of your labours has been to compile, refine and reduce maps of other geographers to folio-sized pages.

Printed as a collection of single-sized maps, historical narratives and source references, your *Theatrum* contains a detailed description of the world like none before it. It will be remembered as a summary of the geography of our century. Your mapbook can be bought at a relatively small cost, kept in a small space and even carried about wherever its owner pleases.

And by your work you have placed Antwerp right in the middle of the cartographic world. You have bettered the Italian mapmakers in the uniformity in size and consistency of style of your maps, and in placing far more emphasis on the explanations in the texts of your mapbook. From now on, your city on the Scheldt will be the leader in cartography as well as in commerce, printing and the arts.

And I was deeply touched by the special homage you paid to me. You called me the prince of geographers of our time. Knowing that you have held Ptolemy in high esteem as the prince of geographers of his time, that is indeed high praise. I thank you for it from the depths of my heart, even though it is hardly deserved.

I remain

Your very assured friend

G. Mercator

10

In his role as Abraham's patron, Gillis Hooftman provided the finance for the printing of *Theatrum orbis terrarum*. He said, 'It was one of the best investments I've ever made, and I'm a pretty shrewd investor.'

One look at his account books and asset sheets would confirm that.

In addition, it surely fixed Hooftman's problem of stacks of maps cluttering his office. Now not only did he have beautiful maps, but he also had tidy maps all in one bound and portable volume.

'Ah, the genius of it!' He sighed appreciatively.

*

Frans Hogenberg engraved most of the copper plates for the *Theatrum*. A mighty effort; it was meticulously detailed work that called for a high degree of accuracy with the burin. 'At least you paid well,' he told Abraham.

He had to copy maps that Abraham had collected and corrected. Sometimes, Abraham integrated several maps or parts of maps together to make a new map. And he had to scale them all down to a uniform size that was appropriate for a page of the mapbook, a page that measured roughly the size of a large family Bible.

Hogenberg wasn't the only engraver involved in the *Theatrum*. Joris Hofnagel, Philip Galle and a few others all contributed to the engraving. Once Abraham had the idea in his mind, he wanted to see its fruition in as short a period as possible. To do that, he had to share out the work of engraving.

'What's the hurry?' queried Hogenberg. 'We've got a lifetime to do it, if you were to agree to it.'

Then there was the text on the back of the maps. Abraham was the first to combine descriptive text with maps, text that told the history and geography of the places. He wanted his readers to gain a total view of each area that his maps illustrated.

*

It was Gillis Coppens van Diest who published *Theatrum orbis terrarum,* Theatre of the whole world.

Map collections had been bound into books before this time. The maps had usually been of odd and large sizes and handpicked at special requests of wealthy patrons. Like the one Abraham first did for Hooftman. Abraham said that the Italians were good at this. They had been assembling collections of maps on order for the wealthy for about twenty years: Lafreri maps they were called, after the first person to produce them. However, Abraham's work was different in that his specially redrawn maps were of uniform size and appearance and bound into a book.

The first edition of the mapbook consisted of seventy maps on fifty-three sheets. That's a lot of very detailed engraving. The order of the maps began with the map of the whole world, then moved on round the globe to the four continents of Europe, Asia, Africa and America. Then came maps of large regions, and lastly maps of discrete countries or smaller areas; most of the latter were parts of Europe.

It opened with an illustrated title page that allegorically depicted the five continents as goddesses. Then followed a dedication to Philip II, King of Spain and the Netherlands, and a poem by Adolphus Mekerchius about the title page goddesses. Next, in later editions, came a portrait of Ortelius by Philip Galle. Abraham's own introduction followed; and, again in later editions, the letter of recommendation by Gerard Mercator. Last in this preliminary section was a list of sources for the maps and an index to the mapbook. The main part of the book consisted of the maps themselves with accompanying text on the back of each sheet.

As a postscript in later editions, there appeared a register of place names as they were known in antiquity. A letter by Humphrey Llwyd on the Druids of the Isle of Man, *De Mona, druidum insula...*, was included from the beginning. Finally, the privilege and a closing inscription which gave details of publishing facts.

However, there were no headings delineating these separate parts; they all ran into each other in an undifferentiated style. Sometimes, a variation in font signified a new section.

I was so proud of his mighty work.

11

As well as publishing the *Theatrum orbis terrarum*, Coppens van Diest engraved the title page with a great deal of flair and detail. I was greatly impressed by it.

'The title page identifies and explains the portraits of the continents,' Abraham pointed out. 'But you can see for yourself what they are about if you look with allegorical eyes.'

Its centrepiece is a triumphal arch, a symbol of power, through which you can enter the *Theatre of the whole world.* On the top of the arch and seated between a celestial and a world globe is a woman who represents Europe, Queen of the World, wearing the imperial crown. She holds a sceptre in her right hand, and in her left, a rudder in the form of a cross connected to the world globe to steer the world's affairs. Christian Europe rules the world, both its countries and its inhabitants. She triumphs over the other continents.

Asia, on the left, is a richly gowned and jewelled Oriental princess who holds an incense-burning container in her left hand. She is known for her aromatic spices and pigments.

Africa, on the right, is black and scantily dressed, holding a branch of fragrant balsam. In general, people believe that the black skin of Africans is a result of their closeness to the sun in the equatorial regions. But Abraham questioned that.

At the bottom, on the left of the arch, sits America. It goes without saying that the most unimportant and uncivilised people are at the bottom. America is naked and holds a club in one hand and a skull in the other; she has probably eaten the owner of the skull. Under her hood she has long hair, on her forehead is a gem, and on her right ankle is a bracelet with bells that ring during the rhythmic dances of their religious ceremonies. Her weapons of bow and arrows are near, and behind her is a hammock in which she sleeps.

In the front, on the right at the bottom of the arch, is a bust representing Terra Magellanica or Terra del Fuego. The bottom portion of this figure is not shown, as the land is unknown but referred to as the Great South Land. The flames under her breast indicate it to be a land of fire.

The title page is a fine example of innovative and striking engraving. I say, 'Well done, Coppens van Diest!'

*

It probably didn't cross Philip's mind that Abraham might have had a momentary second thought about dedicating the book to him as the Spanish were engaged in full-on war with our country, not to mention years of imposing the Spanish Inquisition on our people.

But Abraham thought Philip should be honoured by the dedication. The king ruled over a large empire with territories in every continent. His realm was not a single monarchy but a federation of separate states, each jealously guarding its own rights. His authority was often overruled by local burgomeisters and the upper class. It was little wonder that the Spanish were always at war.

War was such a drain on finances. Despite the fact that gold and silver kept pouring in from the new-found South American territories, the king always seemed to be on the brink of bankruptcy. He had to tax and exploit the resources of his empire to keep up with the wars. This was largely one of the causes of revolt in the Netherlands: we Dutch didn't like taxes.

Abraham thought that he ought to send Philip a copy of his work. All the maps of his kingdom in one book. Now that should be useful. Philip could easily carry it around as he did battle with the nations that resisted his advances and those yet to embrace the Catholic faith.

Eventually, Philip II received a copy of *Theatrum orbis terrarum*. It took a year to arrive on his desk. A little annoyed, Abraham told me that his chief minister, Cardinal Espinosa, inspected it for him. Espinosa straight away turned to the map of Spain and searched for his birthplace. In vain.

'Bad luck,' said Abraham.

He also told me that Philip's secretary wrote swiftly to Antwerp asking, 'Please insert the correct name of my birthplace. And when done, send some new copies of the map of Spain to the cardinal, along with two coloured copies of the thus-altered *Theatrum* bound in leather and gilt for the king. Send these things with haste on the fleet that sails to Spain on the next favourable wind.'

'So eventually Philip was happy to give the mapbook his blessing and to recommend it to peoples of all nations,' said Abraham proudly.

*

I hadn't heard of Adolf van Meetkercke, who is more often known by the Latin, Mekerchius. On enquiry, I found that he was an alderman in the local council of nearby Bruges. He was also a linguist and diplomat. Anyway, he wrote a long poem that explained the title page of the *Theatrum orbis terrarum*, a poem about the five women who surrounded the archway. Here's what he wrote about America.

> America is shamelessly naked
> As a barbarian she grows and lives on human flesh,
> This is proved by the bloody head in her hand.
> In the other she has a cudgel which she uses
> To kill people whom she fattens for that purpose.
> Her weapons consist of sharp arrows and strong bows.
> There are feathers in her clothes and hat.
> She also possesses precious stones
> As proved by her forehead, and her legs are embellished
> With resounding bells, a gorgeous ornament.
> And in a net woven from cotton,
> She sleeps between two trees.

And here's what he wrote about the unknown Great South Land, sometimes called Magellanica.

Magellanica is nowadays not known
Except as a place with a head at the straits
Of Magellan, and therefore thus portrayed.
The body has not received a shape
Since nobody as yet has been able to understand
What she is like, savage or civilised,
Only ornated by burning fire.
For when Magellan first came there
He only saw some fire at many spots
And therefore the Spanish in their language
Call it Terra del Fuego.

*

Abraham himself wrote the introduction to the *Theatrum*. It begins with a quote from his hero, Cicero, who once said, 'Humanity came into existence for the purpose of contemplating the world, that world which is nothing but a pinpoint in the immensity of the universe.'

The introduction continues,

Gentle reader, I give you the theatre of the world, on whose stage in a single volume is played out our story, our human history.

I want you to know that geography is the eye of history. So if you can grasp the geography of a place, then you will have an idea of its history. And if you can see maps with certain glasses before your eyes, then what you see will be kept in your memory, make a deep impression and bear abundant fruit. In order to understand our history, and therefore ourselves, we should know about places and events in which lives unfolded, for they are the determinants of who we are. So whenever we think of another part of the world, we have in mind the image that the maps present. Besides, envisaging places unknown to us widens our horizons.

By way of the maps contained in this volume, I will take you, dear reader, on an exciting journey around the whole of the known world. You will see and hear of places far and wide that will open your eyes to the wonders contained in them.

Because I thought it would bring displeasure to the reader to see the reverse sides of the maps bare and empty, I have made a brief statement and historical notes for every map, so that you can remember the history of each place. And I've indicated which authors I have used as references. And thus, the sum of these things is like a shop or business, furnished with all kinds of delicacies. You can dip into it again and again and take from it whatever you desire.

I know that every reader would like to see their native place included in the mapbook. Don't be too disappointed if it's absent, but if you were able to obtain for me a map of your homeland then I would gladly insert it in further editions. I would be extremely grateful for any such contributions.

I hope you enjoy my mapbook.

*

Abraham always aimed to be thorough. It was almost a fault with him. He meticulously recorded the names of all thirty-three cartographers whose maps he had consulted and sometimes copied the whole or portions. And not only that, he listed all eighty-seven cartographers known to him. Everybody who is anybody in the cartographic world.

These names appeared on four pages known as the *Catalogus Auctorum,* the catalogue of authors, in the initial section of the *Theatrum.* Abraham hoped to make a great contribution to history and to truth, for many other cartographers didn't bother to acknowledge their sources.

*

Known as *Index Tabularum*, the table of contents listed, as might be guessed, the fifty-three sheets of maps that followed in the mapbook. Place names were contemporary.

The maps were carefully selected from the best available. They were logically organised to represent in descending size firstly the whole world, then the continents, followed by regions and political entities, and, in later editions, even details of some specific islands or bays, like the sheet that contained small maps of six of the Mediterranean islands: Corsica, Sicily, Corfu, Malta, Elba and Zerbi. Thus each group of maps revealed more detail of the area shown.

I began to realise that Abraham's geographic thinking and way of going about things, including the ordering of maps in his mapbook, was based on Ptolemy's studies. Abraham informed me once again, as if I hadn't taken it in the first time, that Ptolemy lived in the second century in Alexandria in Egypt, which at that time was part of the Roman Empire. Alexandria had an immense library.

'Ptolemy's work was much broader than merely the subject of geography,' he went on. 'It was lost during the time of the barbarians and only became known again in the past two centuries.'

So now I know that Ptolemy believed that the earth was a sphere, a fact only rediscovered when Magellan circumnavigated the earth. And that Ptolemy used coordinates to pinpoint locations: he marked lines of exact latitude and assumed longitude. His maps had a north orientation and a scale of distances. His work encouraged explorers to go beyond the then known borders of the world.

12

By far the greatest portion of the mapbook was the section containing the maps themselves and their accompanying historical and geographical descriptions.

*

On a damp and foggy morning in May, Mother and I were given a personal audience with his newly completed mapbook.

'I want you to be the first to see this important map, Mother,' he said. 'I've called it *Typus orbis terrarum*, a map of the whole world. Imagine the whole world at your fingertips on a piece of paper. Mercator always considered that the first map occurring in the first regular mapbook would be of fundamental significance to the history of cartography.'

'It's so beautiful, dear. I've been waiting a long time to see this marvel.' Mother admired it with moist eyes.

'You see here in this cartouche,' said Abraham, pointing to the bottom of the map, 'I have quoted one of the ancients, the venerable Cicero: "*Quid ei potest videri magnum in rebus humanis, cui aeternitas omnis, totiusque mundi nota sit magnitudo*. Who can consider human affairs to be great, when faced with the eternity and vastness of the entire world."'

'You can't resist Cicero, can you, Abe?' I said.

Abraham ignored me and went on, 'The power to turn our minds to contemplation of God is fundamental to this map. As you know, we must acknowledge that God is central to our world. This is an aspect I have in mind in drawing all my maps.'

'And rightly so,' was Mother's rejoinder. 'God is in all things and Cicero's saying reads like a psalm.'

Abraham continued, 'A world map also holds immense power and importance. It contains visions of the world for sovereigns and explorers alike. Give them a map of the world, so that they can see how much is left to conquer.'

'I'm not sure that I like the sound of that.' Mother looked a little anxious.

'It's all right,' I said. 'Conquests always follow exploration. Europeans are always trying to control the whole world.'

As the title indicates, the *Typus orbis terrarum* represented a portrait of the earth and the oceans that surround it. Unlike his previous eight-sheet map of the world which used a cordiform shape, this one is oval in shape, like those of classical geographers.

'I really liked the heart-shaped one,' Mother said, 'but I'll take it from you that this map is superior.'

Abraham explained to her that in ancient times the globe was divided into three parts, namely Africa, Europe and Asia, as the New World was still to be discovered. But since the discovery of America, a fourth part has been added, and the continent under the South Pole could yet be a fifth part.

Many had drawn more or less accurate maps of the world in the last century, but it was Mercator's recent world map that was the basis of this map. Abraham also consulted Giacomo Gastaldi's world map and Diego Gutierrez's sea charts of the Atlantic. That's how things were done; mapmakers found the best maps possible that suited their purpose and then updated them using the latest knowledge before publishing them.

I pointed out to Mother the billowing clouds that decorate the four corners of the map. A couple of ships sail in the ocean along with some monsters swimming in the sea. The grotesque fish-monsters are quite beautiful. 'Hogenberg is very artistic when it comes to peculiarities,' I said.

Abraham had placed text on the map itself. On one part, the text states that New Guinea has only recently been discovered, but it was uncertain whether it was an island or part of the southern continent. Another part describes a region that the Portuguese called *Psitaci* because of the incredible number of parrots and its equally incredible vastness. Parrot paradise, I call it.

The map shows huge land masses across the top and bottom. While no one really knows what lies in these regions as they are yet to be explored, their existence has been conjectured to keep the globe in balance.

The text on the back of this map highlights the seas around and within the continents. Abraham told Mother how the seas came to be named and about their differing depths. In the text, he points out that some thought that the waters beneath the polar star descended as if rushing into an abyss and disappeared, never to surface again. And he notes the behaviour of tides of various areas and the effects of Mister Wind, called Eolus.

'That's a very whimsical name,' said Mother.

Next, Abraham describes animals and fish that live in the oceans. 'See how I have illustrated a couple of mythical ones on the map itself.'

He lists some of the marine plants, such as coral, pearls, amber and sponges that gave people pleasure.

'Ah yes,' sighed Mother, 'to my mind, pearls make the most exquisite jewellery, and yet they are so simple. I've always dreamed of wearing a hair-comb with a trio of pearls on it, under my cap of course. What does the Bible say about a pearl of great price?'

'I do hope that people find the world map to be an inviting beginning to the maps that are the heart of this publication,' Abraham finished.

'I'm sure they will, my dear.' Then she added, 'I always said that you would go far!'

*

Mercator happened to be in town at this time. After the evening meal, Abraham got out his mapbook and proudly showed it him.

'Have a look, Mercator,' he said, 'at what I've done to your own depiction of Europe.'

'I can see that you have put together this map from my 1554 map of Europe,' Mercator observed. 'And Greenland has come from my 1569 world map. Iceland was also my work. And I can discern my 1564 map of Great Britain on it too. Ortelius, you are certainly a clever man to integrate all of my sources into one beautiful seamless map.'

'And,' Abraham continued, 'Scandinavia comes from the work of Olaus Magnus, and Russia from the Englishman, Anthony Jenkinson. The south-eastern part of this map is based on Gastaldi's first map of Asia of 1559, and parts of the north African coast on Gastaldi's later map of Africa.'

Always cutting, copying, editing and renewing: vital processes in the art of cartography.

Mercator commented, 'Of course the shores of Europe have been known to us for a long time, and well charted by mariners of old. However, much of the north hasn't yet been explored. You have almost intimated the presence of a passage across the north of Europe through to China in the east. Who knows?'

In the text accompanying the map, Abraham described Europe glowingly. On the whole, the air was temperate and wholesome and the land was fertile. With all sorts of grain and wines, and an abundance of wood, it was second to none, but comparable to the best of other regions. Its cities, towns and villages were so pleasant and beautiful.

Mercator added, 'Although it might be smaller than other continents, it could be considered superior to them all, for it's always been more populated than the rest of the world. Its capital was, and always has been, Rome. The Romans were sharp in wit and sturdy of body, which enabled them to subjugate almost the whole known world.'

'You're probably right there,' replied Abraham. 'All ancient writers have highly praised Europe because of the great dominance of the Romans. Not to forget Alexander the Great's empire.'

'And nowadays it is prominent because the kings of Spain and Portugal together rule the four continents of the world,' said Mercator. 'It seems to me that the inhabitants of this part of the world are born with the natural gift and aptitude to govern the others.'

Then Mercator in his usual adept way captured the essence of it all. 'Europe is considered to be a leader among conquering people of all the other nations of the world, most beautiful and far surpassing the rest. Ah yes, Ortelius, we do indeed live in a blessed land. Except for the presence of our Spanish king.'

'Your thoughts, Mercator,' Abraham said, 'are summed up by this pictorial vignette on the side of the map where Zeus, the white bull, is carrying off the maiden Europa. She was so beautiful that the king of the gods wanted her for himself. See how they are both looking back to the lands of Europe: she longingly, he in triumph.'

*

Of course Abraham wanted to share his masterpiece with our English relatives. He left a letter addressed to Emanuel for me to send off.

Dear Emanuel,

I'm sending you a copy of my new work, *Theatrum orbis terrarum*. I hope you get hours of enjoyment from reading it.

I thought you might be especially interested in the map of Asia, particularly as you are a trader and seek to understand the history of places.

Entitled *A new depiction of Asia*, this map is a scaled down version of my own wall map of Asia, which in turn is based mainly on work by the Italian, Gastaldi. I divided Asia into five great empires, which Ann shaded in different hues when she coloured the map. The first four are each governed by a single ruler, the last by a series of different rulers. They are the Muscovite, Tartar, Ottoman and Persian empires, and the rest known as the Indies. China and Japan in the Far East are part of the rest.

The least known of these is, of course, the Muscovite region. Ann suggested that I fill the empty spaces with illustrations of groups of yurts or tents. Aren't they a delight!

Some geographical highlights are contained in the text on the map itself. It shows parts where medicinal rhubarb is found in great quantity and exported, where vases of porcelain are made, where there is a bridge built of marble, three hundred strides long, and where the city of Quinsai in China is located. According to Marco Polo, Quinsai is 100 *mijls* in circumference and has at least twelve thousand bridges. What a city!

While I know that you can read the back of the maps yourself, I'd like to point out some of their features.

In all writings of ancient times, this part of the world was famous because of the Persian, Median, Assyrian and Babylonian kings. But most particularly, much has been written about it in Holy Scripture, since the human race was first created there by Almighty God, betrayed by the devil and fallen, and resurrected and saved by Jesus Christ. As you and I both know well, almost the entire history related in the Testaments, both old and new, took place in this part of the world.

Strabo and Ptolemy both described Asia in past times. No modern writers have described its whole. Marco Polo and Ludovicus Vartomannus have written much about it that they observed by travelling through the area. Some of the Jesuit missionaries have also written about it.

Next comes the geographical description.

Many large and rich islands belong to this continent of Asia, among which are those discovered in living memory: Ceylon, which produces the best cinnamon; and those discovered by the Portuguese: Sumatra, Java the large and the small one, Borneo, Celebes, Palawan, Mindanao, and the Moluccas now famous for the abundance of cloves and spices. Then there is Japan, and part of what is called New Guinea.

As you no doubt realise, vast areas of inland Asia have not been seen yet. Who knows what explorers might find there in the future?

I trust that you will find the *Theatrum* a production worthy of your attention. And would you please show it to those members of the family that are with you, especially Elisabeth. And don't forget to show the maps to young Jacob; he is now old enough to appreciate the little pictures on them at least.

From your cousin,
Abraham

*

And one to his favourite nephew…

To my dear nephew, Jacob.

Although you are still very young it won't hurt you to gain some learning about maps.

I have just produced a book of maps from all over the world. You could have a look at Uncle Emanuel's copy one day when you visit him. However, I'm sending you a single copy of just one of the maps, that of Africa. I've called it *A new map of Africa* because I have updated an older version drawn by an Italian named Giacomo Gastaldi. I thought you might particularly like the sea battle with its clouds of gunpowder smoke that's in a lower corner that I copied from another mapmaker, this time a Spaniard named Diego Gutierrez.

There is still much to be discovered about the interior of Africa. That's why I have filled it with the paths of rivers and drawings of hills along with no end of notes.

You will see that Africa is divided into four main parts: from the north to the south they are Barbaria, Numidia, Libya and the Land of the Negroes. Neither Egypt nor Ethiopia are considered to be part of Africa, but rather of Asia.

The northernmost of these parts, Barbaria, considered the best area, is washed by the Atlantic and Mediterranean seas and bordered by the Atlas Mountains and by Egypt.

Numidia lies immediately south of Barbaria and abounds with dates which is why the Arabs called it Date-bearing region. It is bound on the west by the Atlantic Ocean, on the north by the Atlas Mountains, on the east by the city of Eloacat not far from Egypt, and on the south by the sandy deserts of Libya.

Libya, the third part, is named Sahara, an Arabian word for desert. It begins east of the Nile and extends to the west as far as the Atlantic sea.

The fourth or southern part is called the Land of the Black People, probably because the inhabitants are black in colour or perhaps because the River Niger flows through the region. *Niger*, as you would already know, is the Latin word for the colour black.

This southern part of Africa was not known until Vasco da Gama first rounded the Cape of Good Hope a mere seventy years ago and came to Calicut in India. So the ancient peoples were not aware of the existence of the Cape. Persians and Arabs first called this southern part Zanzibar.

At the Cape of Good Hope the inhabitants are exceedingly black. Everyone supposes it is the heat and closeness of the sun that causes blackness. However, the sun at the south of Africa is considered no more scorching than at the Straits of Magellan, yet the people there are reported to be white.

So I wonder what causes skin to be black? Is it the heat of the sun? Is it perhaps some hidden property of the soil? Or a quality in the nature of humans themselves? Or is it all of these at the same time?

Mekerchius, the poet, thought that Phaeton was responsible for the blackness of Africans. The Phaeton story went like this: In ancient Ethiopia there lived a youth by the name of Phaeton. His mother was an Ethiopian princess but his father was Helios, the sun-god. Anxious to display his skill in horsemanship, Phaeton asked his father to allow him to drive the chariot of the sun across the heavens for a day. Helios was persuaded by the continued requests of his son and his wife to give way, but the boy was too weak to hold back the horses that rushed out of their usual track. They upset the chariot and caused havoc. Libya was parched into barren sands and all of Africa was more or less damaged, its inhabitants blackened, and the vegetation nearly destroyed. Zeus, god of the sky and king of the gods, killed Phaeton with a flash of lightning and hurled him down into the River Eridanus. Phaeton's sisters, who had yoked the horses to the chariot, were changed into poplars and their tears into amber.

It is a good story, but only a story after all. Blackness of skin is without a doubt a source of mystery to us fair northerners.

From your uncle,
Abraham

*

I was particularly intrigued by the next map, that of America, called the New World. Colouring and decorating it for Abe gave me the chance to get to know and appreciate the detail of this relatively newly known county.

Heralded as a new description of America, the title is contained within a large cartouche topped by a pair of flying lions. The cartouche at the bottom is placed to hide the fact that little or nothing is known of the southern continent that it covered. The horizontal Circle of the Equinox is situated at the centre of the map and lines of latitude and longitude are marked and numbered; the map has an oval shape with decorative corners.

Most of this part of the world has recently been circumnavigated, except for the northern areas, whose coasts have not yet been explored. The shape of America from north to south is in the form of two islands connected by a very narrow piece of land. South America is rectangular in shape and includes Peru, Brazil and Patagonia, the land of giants. The northern part contains New Spain, Mexico, Florida and Terra Nova, known as Newfoundland, in addition to other areas.

At the bottom of the map is the mysterious south land, of which only two points are known: part of the coast of New Guinea and the part known as Tierra del Fuego, the land of fires, that lies south of the Straits of Magellan.

This entire land of America is ruled by the king of Spain, except Brazil, which belongs to the king of Portugal, and Terra Nova, which belongs to the French. So the three major European powers have taken possession of a portion of America each.

I particularly like the name of the two islands called the Unfortunate Ones as they had neither inhabitants nor food.

As always, Abraham acknowledges his cartographic sources. This map was a copy of a portion of Mercator's recently produced world map.

'Mercator gave his permission and encouragement, of course,' he confirmed. 'But it includes place names gleaned from the charts and commentaries of numerous explorers as well.'

Then Abraham wonders how it happened that half of the entire world had been concealed from their ancestors until the time when Christopher Columbus first discovered it. How could it have remained hidden for so long? Even though ancient cartographers had spared no effort in describing the known world, even though the Greeks and Romans had opportunities to explore new regions; and even though the insatiable avarice of humans would use all kinds of trickery to lay their hands on the gold that abounded in this land, yet it remained unknown until only recently.

Abraham then notes that America contains rich and fertile lands. Among other things, they had provided so much sugar to European countries that now it is found in every kitchen, consumed in great quantities by greedy people. In former days, only apothecaries could get hold of it for the benefit of the sick. And before the Spanish first came, these lands had a total lack of useful animals to assist people. There were no elephants, camels, horses, mules, asses or any other animals that could carry loads or give milk. With one exception: the animal the Spanish call the llama. This sheep of Peru was the size of a donkey and the shape of a camel, and some are reddish in colour.

It was amazing how quickly knowledge of the little-known continent of America has grown, considering that it has been only a lifetime since Columbus discovered the place.

'However, Abe,' I sounded a note of warning, 'time could prove you somewhat inaccurate in your portrayal of America.'

*

Overwhelmingly, the greatest number of maps of individual regions in the rest of the mapbook are of European countries. And of those, at least eight pieces had been taken directly from Abraham's previous map of Europe.

*

My favourite map in the mapbook is that of Russia, Muscovy and Tartary. It is the one I most enjoyed colouring. Geographical features apart, it has the most wonderful illustrations on it. I feel that the illustrations are full of mysterious and exciting stories. You could sit and read it for hours and still be intrigued.

Abraham told me how the Englishman Anthony Jenkinson had travelled around Russia and based much of his 1562 map on his own observations. And characteristically, Jenkinson based the eastern part of his map on that of one previous mapmaker and the western part on another. And of course, Abraham copied it himself for his mapbook.

'You could probably call that poaching,' he said.

I pointed to the top corner of the map. 'See, over here is a marvellous tent called a yurt. It is almost palace-like in its decoration and beauty. And in the centre is a group of yurts along with some people and their camels. Look at the young camel suckling from its mother. How touching is that!'

At the top are two figures, one large and one small. The larger, a priest, consults an idol, the golden grandmother named Zlata Baba, who is worshipped by the inhabitants of those regions, about what to do and where to go. She gives clear answers to those who turn to her, with positive outcomes. How convenient it is to have someone to work it all out for you.

And in another corner are a couple beneath a red flag. The cartouche proclaims that the inhabitants of this region adored either the sun or a red cloth hanging from a pole. Not that you could mistake one for the other. They lived in fortresses, ate the meat of animals, snakes and worms, and had their own language. I can't imagine eating slimy worms.

There are some rocks that have taken shapes of people, cattle, camels or other animals. One was once a group of shepherds and their flocks who were suddenly turned into stone in an amazing metamorphosis, without changing their previous appearance. This miracle took place three hundred years ago.

'Isn't that a great story!' Abraham said, laughing.

Below them is a group of people looking up to a figure in a tree. These Kirgessen people live in troops or hordes. They have a peculiar custom: when a priest performs a religious ceremony, he obtains blood, milk and the dung of beasts of burden and mixes it with dirt. He pours it into a vessel, then climbs a tree and sprinkles it over the people kneeling below. This sprinkling is considered divine. When one of them dies, that person is stowed in a tree by way of burial.

Also on the map is Shamarcandia, once the capital of all Tartary, but now decayed to ruins. Here, Tamerlan lies buried, he who took the ruler of the Turks as his prisoner and abducted him, all bound in golden chains.

'Golden chains!' Abraham exclaimed. 'The place must be abounding in gold. It's hard to believe.'

And in the centre of the map are two men galloping by on horses, one wielding a bow and arrow, the other a large knife, both in a threatening manner.

'You'd better watch out for them,' Abraham warned.

The text at the bottom says that it takes thirty days to travel from Cascara to the border of the empire of Cathay, China. The distance between these borders and Cambala in Africa is a journey of three months. It is hard to imagine places being that far apart.

Beside the title cartouche are two figures wearing the most amazing costumes with pointed hats. One has a long bow. On the back of the map, the text tells that these people wore long skirts and narrow sleeves in the Hungarian manner, and had red boots, very short ones which hardly reached their knees. Abraham thought that Peter Coecke van Aelst would have appreciated them. They belted themselves just above the hips and arranged their belt in such a manner that their belly protruded covering their private parts. They had silver coins, not round but square in shape. Abraham thought they look like fried eggs, but as I said, 'My fried eggs are usually roundish in shape.'

13

After the large map section of the mapbook are a few closing remarks. For the benefit of those interested in the geography of the ancient classical times, Abraham incorporated into later editions of his mapbook a fifty-page register of all the places which occurred in Ptolemy's *Geographica*. This register is known as *Nomenclator Ptolemaicus* or just *Nomenclator* for short.

Abraham dedicated the *Nomenclator* to his good friend, Gerard Mercator.

*

Abraham also included Humphrey Llwyd's short *Treatise on the Druids of the Isle of Man* in his *Theatrum*, even though it had little relevance to anything else in the mapbook. It was a meaningful tribute to a precious friendship.

Abraham had much in common with Llwyd; he often talked about him. 'He was Welsh to the core with a great desire to study the long history of the Welsh people and the Welsh language and to collect artefacts that cast light on life in the past.'

He went on to speak of Llwyd's interest in the Druids. 'The Druids of Wales were a Celtic people who discerned the sacred through nature, through the magic of trees, stones and stars, and who were skilled in astronomy and astrology. Because they kept no written records but rather passed down knowledge through word of mouth, there would have been little knowledge of them had not Julius Caesar written down all he could find out about them in his time in Britain. But it wasn't only the lives of these people that intrigued Humphrey Llwyd. It was whether the Romans occupied the Isle of Man (also known as Mona) or the Isle of Anglesey. The accepted position had been that it was the Isle of Man, but the former was twenty-five English miles from the coast, the latter only one mile. As the Romans had written about walking the channel to the island, it must have been Anglesey that was referred to, not Mona. Humphrey too liked accuracy about historical facts.'

Llwyd had translated from Welsh to English a book in which there was an account of an ancient Welsh sailor discovering a continent on the other side of the Atlantic four hundred years before Amerigo Vespucci discovered America. That set some tongues wagging.

While Llwyd had long carried on a correspondence with Abraham, it wasn't until quite late in his life that he actually met Abraham in Antwerp. Abraham showed him his newly produced map of Asia, which Llwyd admired. Abraham promised to send him a copy, provided he exchanged it for one of Wales. One of the hallmarks of Llwyd's map was a list of place names in three languages: Latin, Welsh and English. Abraham approved.

Unfortunately, Llwyd caught a fever and died shortly before the *Theatrum* was published. Abraham found that Llwyd's Welsh map needed some editing before inclusion in his mapbook, so it missed out on the first edition. However, it was included in subsequent editions.

*

For his individual maps and for the mapbook as a whole, it was important that Abraham managed to gain a privilege. A privilege could be imperial, royal or council, or all three at once. They were granted for a certain number of years. This ensured that both the political and religious content of the book were not deemed to be in error. The privilege was sometimes known as a monopoly or copyright. It prevented other people using his maps or making a similar mapbook for anything up to ten years.

I was there when Gerard de Jode got upset about Abraham's privilege. 'Bother and damnation!' he said. 'Ortelius got in first and gained an exclusive right to publish his work, which means that I have to wait years to produce my compendium of maps. He almost certainly ensured through his connections that I was unable to receive such a privilege. Bastard!'

De Jode really thought that he was a better cartographer than Abraham both in detail and style. He may have been right.

'It looks as if Ortelius always has the edge on me,' de Jode further complained. 'He's younger, better connected to map people, more experienced in business matters, and seems to have attracted a huge following of important people. And what's more, he has omitted me from his list of known cartographers in the *Catalogus Auctorum* part of his *Theatrum*. What have I done to him to make him so vindictive?'

He banged his fist on the table.

*

As is the custom with books today, the final page of the *Theatrum* displays an inscription which gives the title, the author, and other publishing facts. Sometimes, an illustration of an emblem of the publisher appears. Plantin mostly used one of the variations of his golden compass in this situation, but Abraham's emblem was a globe circumscribed with the words, *Contemno et orno, mente, manu*, I scorn and adorn with my mind and my hand. This motto summed up his values of not putting too much faith in worldly matters but at the same time creating the world through his maps.

'And while I'm on the subject of Plantin,' said Abraham, 'perhaps I should explain why he wasn't the printer of my major work, even though he supplied the paper for it. It was at a time when he was engrossed in printing the *Biblia Regia*, a polyglot Bible, for the Spanish king and so he had little or no time to devote to me, his dear friend. He did, however, print all of the editions that appeared after 1579.'

14

Practically as soon as *Theatrum orbis terrarum* had been published, Abraham began receiving complimentary letters about it. I had the task of keeping his correspondence in order. I kept all the letters in a special box of inlaid woodwork, such did I treasure them. Some bits and pieces from the correspondence included:

'All extol your *Theatrum* to the skies and wish you well for it. I shall live a worshipper of your name.'

'Your maps have been everywhere of service to us. As we travelled from town to town we paid great attention to them and noticed their defect signified very little, but no correction is wanted.'

Johann Vivianus wrote a poem in which he said the *Theatrum* was like a breath of fresh rose-scented air. High praise indeed.

But not all of the letters were so positive. One disgruntled reader wrote, 'The map of Meissen is not worthy of your work; there is no art in it, and the courses of rivers and the sites of places don't often agree with the lie of the land. Similar errors are found in the map of Saxony. The original author has put many things into his map just as others told him to, with little critique on his part, or indeed on your part in using his map.'

Many responded to Abraham's plea for them to send him maps of areas not covered in the mapbook.

*

The *Theatrum* was an immediate and spectacular success, despite its hefty price tag. Even Abraham was surprised at the way it sold. There were four reprints in the first year of its publication. Because it did so well and because he was so careful about keeping it up to date and accurate, whenever new geographical or historical information came in Abraham revised the maps accordingly. Practically as soon as it was off the press, he began to modify coastlines, add new place names and verify and add source references.

People could buy separate individual sheets if they wanted to, rather than the whole mapbook.

There were fifty-three sheets of maps in the first edition. Abraham took the advice of others and added new maps as were suggested to him. By 1573, he had included seventeen supplementary maps in a section called *Addimenta* (Humphrey Llwyd's map of Wales was among them). Maps, maps and more maps were added in a further four *Addimenta* over the years.

Although the first editions of the *Theatrum* were in Latin, in the following few years the text was produced in Dutch, French and German languages, again so that ordinary people could read it. Later, Spanish, English and Italian versions were also produced.

Overall more than seven thousand copies were produced. It made Abraham a wealthy man.

*

King Philip II of Spain needed to be sure of Abraham's religious affiliation before bestowing on him the title Royal Geographer. He couldn't have a heretic in such an honourable position, so he sent an agent of the Inquisition, Father Arias Montanus, to check him out, little knowing that he was already a good friend of Abraham.

Despite being both Spanish and an Inquisitor, Montanus was a straightforward and mild-mannered Benedictine monk who wore plain priestly garb with a sense of purpose despite a habitually unpressed collar. He also wrote religious poetry and spent a lot of time in prayer. I liked Father Montanus, who, unlike some, always included me in the conversation.

Father Montanus happened to be in Antwerp anyway, preparing a new edition of the Bible at the request of King Philip II. It was a polyglot Bible, one that showed the text in different languages printed side by side. The basic languages he used were Hebrew, Aramaic, Latin and Greek. On the king's orders, Montanus had to take it to Rome to be approved by the Pope. It was printed by Christopher Plantin of Antwerp. Plantin was another who became a good friend to Montanus while he was living here.

Abraham told me that someone objected to the new Bible and denounced Montanus, the Inquisitor, to the Inquisition in Rome. 'He was accused of altering the Biblical text,' said Abraham, 'and, in so doing, disregarded the Council of Trent, which decreed that the Latin Vulgate translation was the only authentic version of the Bible. This was despite the fact that Montanus had been present at the Council of Trent and his speeches had been well received, even of great distinction, as they said. It took a lot of journeys back and forth to Rome to clear his name but persistence won the day.'

So Montanus was delegated to check out whether this mapmaker was a sincere Catholic or not. Rumours had got back to the king about Abraham's involvement in circles that questioned the dogmas of the different religions, including Catholicism itself. They were probably referring to the humanist group. It reminded Abe of the time that his family had been questioned by the Inquisition when he was a child. The Inquisition never forgets.

'I genuinely admire Abraham Ortelius,' Montanus told me. 'His maps are things of beauty, his *Theatrum* a work of wonder, and he counts as his friends all sorts of artists, engravers, printers, poets and humanists. These are things that I value too. I even made a map of the world once in the manner of Ortelius, with the four winds blowing their breath on to the page, and ships and mythical fish riding the seas. However, my map used a side-by-side double circular projection.'

Montanus told Abraham about his experiences with the Inquisition and between them they sorted out that my brother was still an orthodox and fervent Catholic. What are friends for after all? The Bishop of Antwerp confirmed this, so Montanus was happy to report back to King Philip.

The Duke of Alva, in one of his last official duties as Philip's representative in the Netherlands, conferred the the title of Royal Geographer on Abraham in 1575. The position entailed monetary advantages as well. Philip sent a golden necklace worth nearly two thousand Dutch florins. Not to be outdone, Antwerp, through its treasurer, presented a small goblet crafted from a whole ruby.

Montanus knew that Abraham was happy about the outcome because in later editions of the *Theatrum* he signed himself as the Royal Geographer and dedicated a map to Montanus: a map of Montanus's own beloved Spain, the place of his birth. Actually, a map of ancient Spain, based on the writings of such classical authors as Strabo and Appianus. It had an inset plan of Cadiz, the town from where Columbus set out on his explorations. Abraham dedicated it to 'the excellent theologian Benedictus Arias Montanus, a man well versed in languages, knowledgeable in matters, and with great integrity in life, by Abraham Ortelius in friendship and due reverence'.

Part Three

1571–1598

15

You might think that after the whole world's exultation of Abraham's mapbook, life could only be downhill from there. But no! He spent the rest of his life, learning and creating and editing; always busy, never still.

The production of a companion volume to the mapbook was almost inevitable. Originally, it was Frans Hogenberg's idea. He often talked to Abraham about it.

'Do it,' Abraham said. 'I'll help in any way I can.'

However, it was a couple of years after *Theatrum* had been published that a group in Cologne brought this new production into being. Titled *Civitates orbis terrarum*, Cities of the world, it was a collection of plans and panoramic views of cities that was to complement maps of countries in the *Theatrum*.

Civitates orbis terrarum mirrored *Theatrum orbis terrarum* in many ways. It had a similar title and title page, the same size and layout, the same order of maps, and a combination of map and text.

The collection of drawings for *Civitates* took place over many years. I had long watched on as Abraham gathered materials. 'For use later on, somehow,' was how he put it.

Abraham wasn't involved in the actual assembly of this book except as an advisor, but he helped by acquiring new drawings, and copying and updating existing drawings. *Civitates* was printed in Cologne in Germany, where both the publishers, George Braun and Frans Hogenberg, lived at the time.

Just as Abraham would have liked, *Civitates* was designed to be a popular book, a traveller's compendium that would provide instruction, excite curiosity and uplift the spirit. Even ordinary people liked to enjoy their dreams of travel to exotic places.

The first volume was published in 1572. It was an immediate commercial success and reprinted many times in Latin, German and French. Such was the demand that eventually six volumes were developed over the years. That was five hundred and forty-six city views.

The production of a book of city maps and plans was another worldwide first, and soon it became renowned for its artistic as well as its geographic value.

True to form Abraham told me of another of his colleagues. George Braun was the canon and dean for many years at the small St Maria ad Gradus church next to the Cathedral in Cologne. But he also found time to produce the *Civitates orbis terrarum*.

'He organised the acquisition of the drawings and hired the artists,' Abe said. 'He collected maps and drawings from many places and many artists and wrote the accompanying text of the towns' location, history and commerce. Quite a lot of the text consisted of excerpts from my own text in the *Theatrum*. Why start again? One of the details that Braun himself added to many of the maps were figures in local dress, little groups of citizens in the foreground to add a sense of reality to the highly accurate topographical details.'

Abraham said that Braun believed these maps wouldn't be scrutinised for military secrets by the Turks against whom the Spanish king is often fighting. For Islamic religion forbids them to look at representations of the human form.

Now, isn't that smart thinking?

Frans Hogenberg conceived the idea of the book of city maps and collaborated with Braun in producing the first four volumes as well as being the principal engraver. Hogenberg's task was to help collect the pictures and to engrave the work of different artists onto copper plates. He personally engraved the plates of three hundred and sixty-three of the maps over four volumes. And many of the sheets contained two or more plans or views.

As usual, on some of the maps he added a little light-hearted relief. He included the graffiti on the Poitiers Stone, which they had previously visited. The signatures of nearly all the contributors to *Civitates* were there, with the exception of Braun's.

Unfortunately, Hogenberg died at Cologne in 1590 while still working on the *Civitates* project. Simon Novellanus engraved the final two volumes after Hogenberg's death.

Joris Hoefnagel was one of the artists who provided drawings and engraved the copper plates for *Civitates orbis terrarum*. However, he did more than most of the others, who only contributed a few paintings. Many of his drawings were collected on travels over the years and used for this project. He developed most of the original material for the Spanish and Italian towns. He modified the drawings of many other artists so that there would be some sort of unity in the book. Abraham had sent Joris on journeys around Europe to draw the cities and gather other people's maps and plans for reworking for the production. Sometimes he had sketched places that both of them had previously visited together, and he often surreptitiously included miniature likenesses of them both in his pictures.

Most of the maps were panoramic views showing the geography of each city. The wealth of detail in the images gave an idea of the commercial vitality of each town. Hoefnagel particularly included the status and costume of people from all sectors of society. The tranquil appearance of each city hid the fact that these maps were made at a time when violent religious wars wracked the world.

Hoefnagel painted the view of our own city, Antwerp. 'The Lion of Antwerp and the Steen, the castle built in the middle ages, are symbols of resistance against invaders,' he explained to me. 'You can see the River Scheldt with its ships from many nations bringing riches to the city. Walls and a moat surround the city to protect it. The Lady Cathedral rises majestically in the centre of the city. It was only the interior of the cathedral that was ruined when the Calvinists ran amok, and even that is gradually being restored,' he continued.

Then he pointed out the star-shaped fortress that the Duke of Alva had built when he first came with all his troops to stamp out the heresy of those who believed differently. 'And the lush countryside around the city provides fresh food for its markets,' he concluded.

Most of the cities were in Europe but a few came from further afield, from America, Africa and Asia, especially in the later volumes. Even the tiny island city of Mexico City in the middle of a small lake was included. It had originally appeared in a *Book of Islands* that described the geography of all the islands of the known world with their climate, folklore and history.

A closer look at Venice illustrates a view that was first drawn by an Italian artist. In the map's lower panel were added a ceremonial procession of the Doge and members of the senate of the city, all in their formal dress. And so the political identity of that city was recognised. A wide variety of ships in the picture acknowledged Venice's naval and commercial dominance in the Adriatic. Nearly two hundred buildings, bridges and areas of the city were referenced by number, and many more canals, churches and surrounding islands were identified. A feast for the eyes that reflected the wealth and architectural richness of a most beautiful and powerful city, Serenissima: Venice, the serene.

Philip Galle did his utmost over a long period of time to sell and distribute the books.

16

1577 was the year that Philip Galle redrew all the maps of the *Theatrum* on a much smaller scale and published them in a pocket edition. This made it even easier for ordinary people to carry around, and affordable compared to the rather expensive full-sized *Theatrum*. Naturally, the maps were simpler than the *Theatrum* maps, and without illustrations, so not as stunning in appearance, but nevertheless useful. The smaller size of the maps, they were six by four *duimen*, lost something of their essence, but that was to be expected.

Peter Heyns worked with Galle on this production. It was originally called *Mirror of the world* but became known as the *Epitome*, an abridgement of the *Theatrum*. Heyns did the text, in rhyming poetry; he was good at that. Dutch, French and Italian versions of it were made as well as the usual Latin. The pair published it while we were away in England avoiding the Spanish Fury and its massacres. They didn't get a chance to ask Abraham about it but were sure he would have approved as he was always interested in making publications available in everyone's languages.

'I wasn't at all pleased with their production,' said Abraham. 'I thought they did a less than perfect job of the maps. Maybe I'm too fussy. But I'll fix that in future editions.'

However, *Epitome* turned out to be very popular and sold well.

*

Peter Heyns began his working life as a schoolmaster and rose to be the head of an Antwerp girls' school, School of the Laurel Tree. Eventually, he became dean of St Ambrosius's Guild of Schoolmasters.

He wrote poetry in a new metre that was highly regarded. He also produced various textbooks, particularly a manual for handwriting: the book was based around the alphabet. For each of the twenty-three letters of the Latin alphabet, a new chapter began with a large initial capital that he adorned with *grottesca*.

We were dear friends of the Heyns family and Abraham was godfather to their son, Abraham Heyns. Over the years, in both of their comings and goings, they kept up frequent correspondence by letter.

Heyns belonged to the same circles as Plantin and Abraham and all the rest and became a man of considerable learning and standing in the community. He wasn't afraid to speak out strongly for what he believed, even in the face of censure. Some said he was loud and opinionated.

17

It was late summer in 1575, when trees were beginning to bare their branches to the wind. Abraham left Antwerp with a friend to look into remnants of Roman colonial settlements. Johannes Vivianus had passed through the area many times beforehand and vaguely knew the routes. They set out to explore the archaeology of some of the regions just south of the Netherlands and to learn something of their history. For part of the way, young Jeronimus Scholiers joined them to record their discoveries in writing, as also did Jan van Schille to record them in paintings.

Before they started out, they had to apply to the authorities for permission to travel. They had to prove the necessity of the trip for study purposes and to give a guarantee of return. The Duke of Alva had laid down such conditions for travel.

I had read that, long ago in 51 BC, Julius Caesar had conquered what was then called Gallia Belgica, consisting of the southern Netherlands, Luxembourg, and nearby parts of France and Germany. The Romans built cities, towns and villas in the area. The remains of some of these are still present and have been excavated, along with forts, and tombs of notable people. The tombs look like miniature Roman temples with columned entrances. This was not a mapping exercise at all, just an enjoyable exploration of the ancient history and geography of the region.

I listened with interest when Abe told me the story of this journey when he got home again.

'At a brisk pace, we headed for Mechelen, walking along the edges of lush green lands of crops and cows. Farmers were sickling and scything hay in the fields, frogs croaked in the marshes and midges flew in circles above our heads. Parts of the route followed old Roman roads. Vivianus was always keen to impart his knowledge of history. He told us that long ago, the Germanic tribes round here were converted to Christianity by St Rumbold, an Irish missionary, who was a long way from home. He went on to explain that the Mechelen Cathedral is dedicated to him. As you can see, the tower was never completed to plan. But it has a fine set of bells. If we are lucky, we may hear them chiming. We were both familiar with the city of Mechelin as it was quite close to Antwerp and we had made friends with its many of its printers, painters and illuminators.'

'You didn't stop there to visit any of those people?' I asked.

'No, we needed to get on, so we trekked at a brisk pace onwards to the university town of Leuven, nestled in a low range of hills. The remains of a Roman settlement on the bank of the River Dijle caught our attention before we entered the town through its imposing thirteenth-century city gate. Our humanist friend, the scholar Petrus Divaeus, a magistrate of the city, lived in Leuven. A visit was a must, and after dinner we settled down to a lively discussion of Divaeus's historical works which I, at least, had read. Scholiers, who, along with van Schille, had joined us here at Leuven, unashamedly nodded off to sleep.'

'How embarrassing,' I said. 'I hope you managed to wake him before Divaeus noticed.'

'Yes, but not before a small snore or two managed to escape. Anyway, the next day, we trudged up a steep hill on our way to Gembloux. After catching our breath, we visited the library to see its old books and just enjoy the solitude of the place. It was a lot easier going downhill again through the valley of the Meuse to its junction with the Sambre. The following day dawned bright and sunny with a breeze just strong enough to blow my hat into the water: a perfect day for a boat trip along the Meuse passing many castles on the crests of hills, till we came to the city of Liège.'

'Liège is the place that has a fancy tombstone of John someone or other, isn't it?' I asked.

'We were rather intrigued by that tombstone of John de Mandeville, an Englishman who had written an account of his extraordinary travels to the east in the fourteenth century, which I had enjoyed reading. De Mandeville had died at Liège and was buried in the church of St William. Van Schille recorded his coat of arms, while Scholiers recorded the Latin inscription on his stone, saying that it said de Mandeville was a professor of medicine and often known as *ad Barbam*, because of his long beard that came halfway down to his waist.'

'He would have looked liked an old goat,' I said, laughing.

Abe went on. 'Van Schille also drew an outline of the carving on the tombstone: an armed man with a long forked beard, stepping on a lion, and asked whether perhaps the lion was a barbary lion and maybe meant to symbolise Mandeville himself.'

'Could be, and perhaps more likely than a goat,' I said.

Liège was also a place where several of their friends lived. They visited Dominicus Lampsonius, with whom Abe had corresponded with over the years. Abraham fondly patted him on the back and said that it was good to see him face to face at last.

'Lampsonius liked to paint and write verses,' he continued, 'as well as undertaking linguistic studies. He was indeed versatile. I first began to correspond with him in order to get my hands on some English maps when Lampsonius was secretary to the Archbishop of Canterbury in England.'

'You certainly went to great lengths and many people to get your maps, Abraham,' I said.

'Perhaps the most pleasurable of our visits was an evening we spent with Arnold de Wachtendonck, an expert in local history. We delighted in his collection of coins, antiquities and lavishly illustrated manuscripts. From Liège, we embarked on a detour to Tongeren, once a Roman provincial capital. There, we wandered around some remains of the defensive walls that used to surround the place, and some old and decrepit mound graves in the neighbourhood. On the journey to and from Tongeren, we shared tales of Caesar's first century campaigns in the area, and of the sometimes successful revolts of the locals against him. Vivianus remembered the story of Caesar's foe Ambiorix the rebel. In his pursuit of Ambiorix, Caesar invited Germanic tribes to come and plunder the local villages, so that he wouldn't have to lose any more troops in the fighting.'

'A crafty old coot was that Caesar! And a crafty way to trap his opponent Ambiorix,' I said. 'I can just imagine Ambiorix falling into that trap. I do like that story.'

Abraham continued. 'Soon we reached the woods of the Ardennes, all decked in autumn glory and stroked by the sun's rays streaming through the branches of the trees. It was pleasant walking, even if steep or rough in parts. We liked the crunch of autumn leaves beneath our feet, but weren't so keen on the smelly rot of them in places. I stopped frequently to inspect the back of the silvery leaves of a poplar with my lens and to find intricate patterns in the yellow centre of a daisy. I looked into hollows of tree trunks to see if there were any nesting birds. The tranquil forest with its toadstools on the mossy floor and shrill birds in the leafy canopy always revives the soul. A stop at Spa for a refreshing wallow in the sparkling bubbles of the spring water was followed by a meal of rustic bread and sharp cheese.'

'I would have liked to be with you on that part of the journey. It all sounds so beautiful,' I said.

'We stopped at the abbey at Stavelot, pausing for some quiet reflection in front of the glorious altar backed by a splendid golden triptych and containing a relic of the original cross. Continuing after passing through several small townships, we soon came to Luxembourg. There, our group stopped to visit Joannes Moflinius, another friend, from whom I acquired manuscript maps and paper while he was employed as a chaplain at the Spanish court. Moflinius introduced us to his current employer, Count Ernestus, the governor of Luxembourg. So we had a good day inspecting the count's collection of Roman statues and monuments, recording inscriptions and listening to his learned tales of Roman history. Moflinius took us in his carriage to visit the remnants of a Roman vicus in the neighbourhood. An unplanned settlement built to profit from Roman troops in the area, it had offered supplies and entertainment, even harlots, for the soldiers. At the end of the day, after an excellent meal of braised fowl, we slept in real beds. We needed to make haste to Nancy, it was still three days away. We didn't stop along the route as I had heard that there was plague in those parts.'

'I'm glad you kept away from plague-ridden towns. It simply wouldn't do for any of you to get ill,' I said.

'It was still mild enough to spend the night in the open air under a tree – beside a small fire, of course. Vivianus commented that Nancy was the place where Charles the Bold, Duke of Burgundy, died nearly a hundred years ago. What a horrible man he was. It was bitterly cold at the time of the Battle of Nancy, cold enough to lose many troops to frostbite. They killed him and threw his naked and disfigured body into the river, where it was discovered several days later, frozen. Van Schille, who knew the story too, was able to add that his head had been cut in two by a halberd and lances were lodged in his stomach and loins. His face had been so badly mutilated by wild animals that they could only identify him by his long fingernails and the old battle scars on his body. Scholiers considered that was a fitting end to a man who ordered his troops to destroy the city of Dinant, killing every man, woman and child within. We caught a ride on a small sailing boat from Nancy down the Moselle to St Nicolas de Port. Its sails were taut in the wind, so we moved quickly, giving our feet a bit of a rest. Through the clouds, we could see the twin bell towers of the Basilica of Saint Nicolas soaring above the surrounding houses long before we actually reached it. The church contained a shrine for a relic of St Nicolas: one of his fingers was brought back from the Crusades, a finger that is supposed to have caused miracles.'

'Agh, how barbaric,' I groaned

'Relatively recently, in the 1400s,' said Abraham, 'St Nicolas was built in all its glory with an elaborate western front, intricately ribbed vaulting and colourful stained-glass windows. We felt like pilgrims of old, but we had come to admire a building, rather than a mouldy old finger. Heading a little way up river to Metz, which had been an important town in Caesar's time, we found several entire arches remaining of the Pont Jovy, a Roman aqueduct which once crossed the Moselle from one mountain to another. Vivianus added that this was where country people of the neighbourhood supposed that it was a real bridge and that the devil had built it. Then I asked Scholius to make a sketch of the arches. At last we came to the village of Igel. There, we gazed in wonder at a very tall sandstone column: a burial monument of a wealthy Roman cloth merchant from around AD 250. It had a decorated bas-relief showing the home life of a Roman family: a family sitting around a table drinking, while servants poured the drinks from ewers, washed the dishes and prepared a meal. Scholius presumed that they ate the goat, the eel, the rooster and the basket of fruit that are also incised into the sandstone.'

'Not so different to what we eat,' I said.

Abe continued, 'Anxious for the job to be done properly, I asked Scholiers to also copy the inscription that accompanied that domestic bliss and van Schille to sketch the column so we could make a wood block of it when we got home. Such an illustration would surely add something to our notes. Even more amazing old buildings were awaiting us at Trier. I'd been there before and was anxious to show the others the remnants of the cloisters of St Paulinus and Latin gravestone inscriptions at the Abbey of St Maximin. Nearby at Echternach we admired an eleventh-century illuminated book of the Gospels, the *Codex Aureus*, which was meticulously produced by monks at the local monastery and kept in their library. It was lavishly illustrated with pages of carefully drawn figures and rich colouring that included a lot of work in gold leaf. While later than Roman in origin, it was a most beautiful book. And your map colouring, Ann, is almost as beautiful. I'm lucky to have such a talented sister,' said Abraham.

'But on with the story. It was a short walk from Echternacht to the river. We managed to catch a barge for the long trip to Koblenz. The city of Koblenz was located on both sides of the Rhine, where it met the Moselle. The Romans built a large arch-shaped bridge of stone across this part of the river. It was still visible. Then they built two strong forts crowning the hills and circling the town as protection for the bridge, although only one of the forts remained. And just north of Koblenz was a fine-looking temple dedicated to Mercury and Rosmerta, Gallo-Roman deities. As we were anxious to get to Frankfurt in time for the annual book fair, we left next morning in the grey dawn and arrived at our destination by the light of the full moon. We had been journeying for two months by this time and were glad of a lengthy period in Frankfurt. First thing we did on arrival was to find a cobbler and get our boots mended, or in Vivianus's case to get some new boots. As he threw his old ones onto a rubbish pile, he reckoned his feet would be glad to be rid of his smelly and holey pair.'

'What a long and interesting trip that was,' I said. 'I bet you were glad to get home by the end of it.'

*

Nearly ten years later, Plantin published a travel report of this journey in the form of a letter to Gerard Mercator: *Itinerarium per nonnullas Galliae Belgicae partes,* A journey through some parts of Gallic Belgium. Included were some woodcut illustrations, but no maps.

It sold well, but most importantly, Mercator was delighted with it.

'It contains valuable information about the old geography of Belgium but would be especially important to those who study the languages and archaeology of ancient cultures,' he said. 'Thank you Ortelius. I am truly touched by this gift.'

18

Numismatics, or collecting ancient coins, was a popular pastime of the time. Like Abraham, Hubert Goltzius was besotted by coins of bygone days and far-off places. In one study trip across the continent, Goltzius visited nine hundred and seventy-eight coin collectors and numismatic scholars. It was a two-year trip, funded by a newly found patron. He listed all of the collectors and scholars in an appendix to one of his books on the subject. The list could have been a book in itself.

I rolled my eyes as Abraham launched into yet another background story.

'Goltzius had come to Antwerp and joined the Guild of St Luke in 1546. His sister married Peter Coecke van Aelst and so it was through Peter that Goltzius came to meet other artists in Antwerp. He also painted, made woodcuts and prints, etched and engraved. He engraved the weeping mother of Jesus in the *Pietà*. It seemed that everyone drew, painted or sculpted the pietà: it was a popular subject. In Antwerp, Goltzius made a living dealing in art and antiques. He taught me a lot about coin collections and told me how to obtain more customers for my own business. He was a perfectionist with a voracious appetite for work and his seriousness was reflected in his furrowed brow and gaunt features.'

I actually feel that I'm part of Abraham's whole endeavour when he tells me these stories of his confrères.

In Antwerp, Abraham introduced Goltzius to the humanist circle that he belonged to. Goltzius especially enjoyed the discussions that involved ancient and classical times and works.

Goltzius made drawings of coins and medals and began a system for their classification. After his study trip he produced a book of great beauty, *Vivae omnium fere imperatorum imagines...*, Images of almost all the living emperors from Julius Caesar to Charles V..., that contained portraits of ancient emperors done in a cameo technique. The illustrations of the medals were slightly larger than seven *duimen* in diameter and printed with several ink colours. The title page had to be printed in two stages, one for the engraved text and one for the woodcut illustration. Complex printing. It was published in three languages.

'Of course, I bought a copy for my library, and one for my young nephew in London,' said Abraham.

Goltzius told Abraham that he had once circulated a letter on leaving decisions about religion to the state councils rather than to particular churches. It wasn't a clever thing to do, but he felt he had to, in freedom of conscience. 'As Cicero said, "The greatest theatre for virtue is conscience,"' Goltzius said. 'In the wake of all that, I deemed it auspicious to leave Bruges till the storm had passed.'

Goltzius moved to Bruges in 1562. There he wrote *Julius Caesar*, a history of the life of Caesar with full-page engravings of ancient coins showing his image within ornamental frames. Ten years later, he produced its sequel, *Caesar Augustus*.

*

Philip Galle moved back to Antwerp from Haarlem after it was besieged for seven months by Spanish troops.

Abe was quick with yet another potted history. 'In Haarlem, where he was born, Galle had been a pupil of Dirck Coornhert in the art of engraving. When Galle first came to Antwerp, he joined the Guild of St Luke and was employed in the workshop of Hieronymus Cock, who published his first set of prints. Galle was both a designer and an engraver, and specialised in engraving paintings, including some by Bruegel. Later, he began engraving maps as well, even though in the beginning he found them difficult to master. Soon he was able to set up his own publishing and print business back in Haarlem. He found it necessary to travel to both obtain and sell material. It was many years beforehand that he toured much of Europe and met up with Mercator, Hoefnagel, Hogenberg and me at Poitiers where we had all signed the rock. After Hieronymus Cock died in 1570 and bequeathed his presses to Galle, Galle came back to Antwerp. Soon, his portly waistline showed evidence of his success.'

In Antwerp, Galle's house, *Het gulden hert*, The golden deer, was opposite ours, so we got to know him as a neighbour and a friend, and he quickly joined Abraham's humanist circle. My brother was also the godparent at the baptism of one of Galle's children.

It was Abraham who got Galle interested in history. He was intrigued by the library in our house. Not only did it contain hundreds of books and maps but all sorts of other ancient curiosities as well. A veritable museum of wonders.

In 1573, Galle published Abraham's little book *Deorum dearumque capita...*, Heads of gods and goddesses..., a description of his large collection of coins and antiquities. It was lavishly illustrated by Galle's engravings of portraits of the deities.

*

It wasn't until nine years after the mapbook first appeared that Abraham went to Christopher Plantin to publish his continuing new editions of the *Theatrum*. They made a good partnership, selling hundreds of copies over the years. Many of them were sold to the well-to-do middle class who were beginning to take an interest in education and scientific matters. Because of its attractiveness in a book format, it reached a much wider audience than loose maps would ever have done.

Plantin achieved a substantial amount in his professional life as a printer. 'I came to Antwerp in 1548,' he said, 'and published scholarly books of every kind. By the 1570s, I had sixteen printing presses and twenty compositors, thirty-two pressmen and three proofreaders at my beck and call, in addition to the staff for the house and bookshop. Later, the number peaked at a hundred and sixty men who operated twenty-two presses. That's impressive, isn't it?'

Officina Plantiniana became the largest printing house in the whole of Europe. He had to extend his workshops several times. And while he was at it, he included a courtyard garden in the midst of the four wings of his house. 'In the summer of sunshine and blooming roses,' he said, 'it was a good place to sit and talk with my wife Jeanne or with friends, or to watch my grandchildren play. It was quite delightful!'

In 1573, he completed the printing of eight volumes of the Antwerp Bible, as it became known. It was the splendid polyglot Bible prepared by Arias Montanus at the request of King Philip II. It was also known as the Royal Bible. As a result, the king appointed Plantin as Royal Architypographer, in charge of printing all the king's breviaries, missals and psalters. They were sent to Spain in great numbers at the expense of the king. So Plantin acquired a very lucrative deal which in turn allowed him to become Europe's leading printer of humanist, scientific and religious books.

This monopoly happened to be the incidental cause of him printing sheet music. When King Philip withheld a subsidy promised for a luxurious book of antiphons, Plantin found that he had to find a use for the eighteen hundred reams of special-sized paper already ordered, so he issued a volume of sung masses. During the following decade, he made the publishing of sheet music one of his specialties.

He published many new editions of the classics, works on legal theory and an index of works forbidden by the Council of Trent. Later, wars stopped him producing the new liturgical books that had been ordered by the king; but he had, long before, obtained privileges for this work from Rome. An exclusive privilege for two hundred years became a great source of profit and compensated for the losses incurred by the Royal Bibles, which King Philip had difficulty in paying for once he had them in hand.

'I published works of some authors who were considered heretics,' Plantin explained. 'I had to be very devious in doing it so that they couldn't be connected to me in any way. I even had to flee to France for a couple of extended periods as a result, just for safety. I had to be sure that I emphasised, in every possible way and with monotonous regularity, in any letters that I wrote to my Spanish contacts, what an orthodox Catholic I was.'

Over a thirty-year period, he produced nearly two and a half thousand different titles, which were distributed via Paris and Frankfurt as well as Antwerp. His editions often consisted of as many as fifteen hundred copies and, occasionally, considerably more. He printed nearly four thousand copies of the Royal Bible.

Plantin also printed works by locals, among them, de Jode, Goltzius, Galle and Heyns as well as Abraham. He printed works by scholars from all over Europe who brought their writings for publication.

For many years, Plantin was still owed twenty thousand florins by the king for contracts for which payment didn't materialise. He had to labour long hours to make up for the loss, and nearly became insolvent in the process.

19

Philip Galle was living in Antwerp when the Spanish soldiers marched into the city in 1576 and began massacring people and burning houses in what was to become known as the Spanish Fury. Being a peace-loving person and utterly terrified, he had made sure he didn't get involved in events but stayed shut away in his house hoping that it wouldn't get attacked. 'But,' he told us later, 'I could see out of my window how cruelly the Spanish soldiers were killing people right, left and centre, women and children as well. Shooting them, hacking them down with their halberds and even throttling them. They didn't stand a chance. Blood was everywhere. Moaning and dying bodies were lying in the gutters.'

He stopped to wipe his eyes and get his breath back before continuing. 'Hysterical screams filled the air along with gun shots and sounds of raucous laughter from the Spanish soldiers. It was absolutely horrific!'

I remember well that dreadful time. The smell of smoke and roaring of the fires were everywhere. It was distressing for us all. The Spanish soldiers looted and set fire to public buildings. From our house, we could see flames leap high into the air devouring everything in their path. But we, like everyone else, didn't dare to venture out to extinguish them. The pungent smoke got up our noses and fine flying ash into our eyes.

The new city hall was burnt so that only the exterior walls were left standing. It contained many irreplaceable art treasures. Then they started destroying well-to-do houses in the city. We were afraid for our lives and hid in the cellar. For three days it went on, unrelentingly. About a third of the town's buildings were flattened or burnt.

While our house was out of the danger zone, we were still greatly affected by such wanton destruction. What could we do anyway with only buckets? It would have been futile to try.

Afterwards, Galle wrote a long letter to a friend telling him all about it. It was published and translated into several languages. 'I thought it was important for personal accounts to be written of such historical atrocities,' he said, 'so that future generations could know first-hand how utterly awful it was.'

*

The Spanish soldiers were pretty well leaderless. Alva had been recalled and Requesens was still on his way to take his place. Angry at fighting without rest or pay, the soldiers had already destroyed two other towns. Word was that they were sick of waiting for their pay that was coming on a ship from Spain. A storm had blown up in the Narrow Sea, the ship was delayed and sought shelter in an English port, of all places. The English seized the 400,000-florin pay packet that was on its way to Antwerp. The English hated the Spaniards as much as we Dutch did. The hungry soldiers couldn't wait any longer in the wealthy city of Antwerp, so they decided to help themselves.

Violence was such as had never been seen before. More than seven thousand people were massacred and a great deal of property was destroyed or just taken. Antwerp was in chaos.

Joris Hoefnagel told how the Spanish Fury affected his family. 'When the Spanish soldiers went on their rampage through Antwerp in the Spanish Fury, they pillaged everything my father owned, took every last diamond and ruby, burnt the house down and left our family seemingly for dead. Needless to say, we quickly got out of Antwerp to safety in Munich in Germany.'

Christopher Plantin was only able to save his printing establishment by paying a huge ransom to the soldiers. In fact, over the years, Plantin had to pay a ransom to rescue his property seven times.

How does one write about such unspeakable atrocities? Frans Hogenberg wasn't in Antwerp at the time of this Spanish Fury but he heard about it from one of Galle's letters that had been published for all to read, and he was appalled. He refrained from writing about it; he drew it all. He got out his burin and engraved seven impressions of the horror in Antwerp. He was familiar enough with the city to be able to render a fair likeness.

After this, he began work on news-sheets illustrating political events. He engraved a whole series of scenes from the Spanish wars in various parts of Europe.

Abraham's friend, Hans Collaert, also engraved the destruction. His engraving was an allegorical statement about the horror. In the centre of this work was the tree of life. At the top, God looked down from the sun. On one side, Patience, with the cross in her hand and the lamb of God on her knee, sat amid the devastation of war. Beside her, the dead were being buried. In the background, the soldiers ran amok and burnt the city hall, representative of all the buildings that were razed. On the other side, Poverty, with a severed foot, defended his hungry children. In the idyllic rural background, a peasant couple pleaded for mercy in the face of attacking soldiers. For the Spanish, there was no difference between the rich and poor; all were targets of their wrath.

Perhaps Collaert was a bit optimistic in his depiction of the whole Dutch world waiting long-sufferingly, but not too hopefully, for peace and religious freedom to become a reality.

Abe wondered what Peter Bruegel would have made of the Spanish Fury, had he still been alive.

And how did our family cope with all of this?

'Get ready quickly!' Abe demanded of Mother and me. 'The Spanish have rapidly taken over the whole of Antwerp and have left a trail of destruction behind them. Let's get out of here and go to our London family. Don't pack too much, just a few of our more valuable things. And while you're doing that, I'll go down to the wharves and see if there's a ship sailing tonight.'

A storm was brewing. Lightning erupted from black rolling clouds, the westerly wind rose to a howl. Hardly sailing weather, thought Abraham as he battled the wind along the cobbled streets to the wharf. There, he found just a single ship, her sail lines thrumming in the wind and mooring hawsers straining at the bollards. Greasy workers hurled their last bales of wool on board and secured the hatches.

'Sailing to London tonight. Trying to beat the rain,' barked the captain when Abraham asked his intentions.

'Could you possibly squeeze in three passengers? My mother and sister are slight in size. We will pay you well.'

'There is nowhere to sleep on this ship that would suit the likes of you. You'll have to take your luck and find some spaces in the hold among the bales. You won't even be able to lie down. And you'll have to be quick about it as we're sailing within the hour.'

When it was all over, we found that our house in Antwerp hadn't even been touched. What would the Spanish want with a lot of old books and coins anyway?

20

We stayed in London for several months.

Our brother-in-law, Jacob Colius, had been naturalised as an Englishman in 1568, so his family were destined to settle in England forever. They had moved to the southern end of Lime Street in London, near where Emanuel van Meteren lived.

Our nephew, the younger Jacob Colius, the one born in Antwerp in 1563 and known as James Cools to the English, had been able to study Latin and Greek. For the previous couple of years, Abraham had been writing simple letters in Latin to him and sending him books.

'I really enjoyed translating your letters,' Jacob told his uncle. 'They were interesting, for they were about ordinary family things, not battles and mythical wanderings like the Latin of my classical studies. And the books you sent me were about things that we both share an interest in: birds and trees and flowers, history of the ancients, old coins and fossils, and other curiosities. My mother said that I gained as much education through your correspondence as I did from school.'

It was good to catch up with family again. And Abraham was anxious to take the opportunity to meet some of England's geographical experts. Wasn't he always on the look out for new knowledge and a profitable deal on more maps?

*

Emanuel van Meteren and his family lived in London throughout the reign of the red-headed Queen Elizabeth. She had succeeded to the throne in late 1558 and seemed to reign for ever, longer than most sovereigns in those days.

While we were in London in 1577 Emanuel and Hesta welcomed

us into their house for a short while. We stayed with each of the other family members for a few days and caught up with everyone, especially any new children that we hadn't yet met. How Abraham loved little ones. He would sit and talk to them for hours, telling them stories and singing them to sleep.

While he was there, Abraham travelled around both England and Ireland. The money he had received from the publication of *Theatrum* allowed him to go where he wanted.

Emanuel was able to introduce Abraham to many geographers and cartographers in England, where he was quite well known since the publication of the *Theatrum*. People were just as eager to meet him as he was to meet them. He was particularly interested in meeting with the scholars John Dee, William Camden and Richard Hakluyt.

*

Early on a cold and drizzly morning, Emanuel hired a two-horse carriage and took Abraham and his maps along the cobbled streets to John Dee's house in Mortlake on the south bank of the Thames, where Dee had arranged for Abraham to meet William Camden and Richard Hakluyt. Emanuel promised to return to pick him up at dusk.

If I had been a fly on the wall, I could almost have taken part in this meeting. I would have seen the four men sitting comfortably around a newly laid fire which soon settled into a glow of coals and added to the candle light. And I would have heard their animated conversation, each trying to outdo the other. The one thing that each had in common was their love of maps and all that their maps signified. They all valued maps above almost anything.

'It's good to catch up with you again, my old friend.' Abraham had met John Dee when Dee had visited Antwerp in 1550. 'It's been a long time but we've kept up a correspondence.'

'And you've sent me many good books to augment my library,' said Dee. 'I think my library might be bigger than yours by now,' he chuckled. He certainly had a vast collection of manuscript documents dating back hundreds of years. He took pleasure in mathematics, astrology and magic, navigation and cartography. Put a medieval pointed hat on his head and a colourful cloak on his shoulders and he might be mistaken for a wizard with his long pointed beard.

'Allow me to introduce you to these two young men who both have an obsession for maps like we do,' said Dee. 'Firstly, this is William Camden. He's been working at Westminster school in London. It's a position that suits him as it allows him the freedom to travel and pursue his antiquarian research during school breaks. And secondly, meet Richard Hakluyt. He's still studying at Oxford University, concentrating on geography and navigational technology.'

'Pleased to meet you both,' said Abraham warmly shaking their hands. 'I've known for some time that Hakluyt has an interest in the New World, so I've been corresponding with him to clarify some place names along the American west coast for my *Theatrum*. Come and see what I've brought for you perusal.'

They moved to the library and quickly settled down to thumb through the strikingly coloured folios of the *Theatrum*.

As Hakluyt opened to the page of the American map, he said hesitatingly, 'I've always been fascinated by the stories of Martin Frobisher searching for a north-west passage across the top of America and into the Pacific Ocean to China.'

Abraham pointed to the relevant position on his map of America. 'You may have noticed that I too hinted at such a possibility on this map. Had there not been wars going on in my part of the world for so long, we Dutch would have been up there looking for the north-west passage long before Frobisher. I believe he's up there at the present with his little ships.'

'What exciting news,' said Dee.

'It is indeed,' added Camden.

Encouraged by their interest, Hakluyt spoke more about Frobisher's journey. 'After spending ten years dreaming about it and five years gaining some funds for his trip, Frobisher's first attempt didn't come to much in the way of discovering a north-west passage. His was a perilous journey through the bone-chilling ice and howling wind of the north Atlantic. Eventually, he arrived at a large bay in the remote Arctic. He thought he had discovered the entrance to the passage. But it was there that five of his crew were kidnapped by the natives, so Frobisher felt it was time to come home.'

'Wise man!' Abraham exclaimed.

'He then found tons of gold, or what he thought was gold. He was so excited that he loaded some onto his ship and brought it home,' said Hakluyt. 'But it turned out to be fool's gold, worthless pyrites.'

'Easy enough to mistake,' Abraham commented. 'I'm sure I wouldn't know the difference on first sight either.'

Dee interrupted. 'While I've been employed as adviser to Queen Elizabeth on astrological and scientific matters,' he said, 'I've had the opportunity to guide promoters of such voyages, including Frobisher, and to provide them with navigational assistance.'

'A work of great importance,' said Hakluyt.

'And it was me who coined the term "British Empire",' continued Dee. 'I have long advocated the development of such an empire when setting up colonies across the Atlantic. Have any of you seen my newly published work yet?' he asked, picking up a copy of *General and rare memorials pertaining to the perfect art of navigation*.

'No, not yet,' said Abraham, 'but I'm looking forward to reading it. It must be very recent.'

'It is. It was published just last month. Despite its seemingly unrelated title, it explains my vision for a British maritime empire,' Dee said. 'And I created the title page myself, showing Elizabeth at the helm of her ship in charge of Britain's imperial destiny.' Opening to a book-marked page, he continued, 'Here, I point out in some detail why England has territorial claims on the New World over and above the Spanish. In support of those claims, I've included Humphrey Llwyd's hypothesis that it was a boatload of Welsh men who first sailed across the Atlantic and settled there four hundred years ago.'

'I'd be interested in reading what underlies Llwyd's thesis about all that. It all sounds a bit far-fetched to me,' said Camden.

They paused long enough to eat some bread and soup that had been prepared for them by Dee's cook.

Settling in front of the fire with a wine glass in hand, Camden took up the conversation. 'I've been thinking about writing and producing a work that is to be a topographical and historical survey of England, Wales and Ireland. I want to restore antiquity to Britain, and Britain to its antiquity. It is to be a study that relates landscape, geography, antiquities and history.'

They were all very interested in Camden's ideas. Abraham was particularly pleased to hear that Camden wanted to include a historical perspective.

'I want to approach it in a different way,' Camden explained. 'Rather than write a history, I want to describe in detail the Britain of the present and show how traces of the past can be discovered in the existing landscape. I want to get to understand Roman Britain.'

They got up to pore over some maps and materials that Camden had collected of Roman London when it was situated on the north bank of the Thames. Each had read about ancient London, so they shared what they knew, compared their sources for consistency and theorised about their differences.

Abraham encouraged Camden to stop dreaming about it and to get started. 'Learn some of the languages that will help, like Welsh and Anglo-Saxon, so you can study any original historical accounts themselves,' he said. 'Travel around, see evidence left by those who have gone before and gather bits of local folklore, for it often contains historical truths.' With a grin, he added. 'Don't put it off any longer. Start now! And call it *Britannia,* there's a grand name for you.'

'Mmm,' Camden thought as he arched his bushy eyebrows to his receding hairline. 'Perhaps I'd better follow my own advice: "The early bird catches the worm."' He liked creating pithy little sayings.

As the afternoon drew into shadowy dusk, and as each gathered up the materials they had brought along, Hakluyt voiced his suspicions. 'I would guess that the chief reason you came to England, Ortelius, was to pry into the secrets of Frobisher's forthcoming voyage. And you probably want to know what is going on with Francis Drake, who is looking to go to America again and try to circumnavigate the earth,' he added. Hakluyt was right of course.

'I'd really like some of your maps of Britannia when you've finished, if you please, Camden,' Abraham added. 'And Hakluyt, could you send me more information about Frobisher as you gather it. And I'll do likewise for you.' Abraham shook hands all round as they left. 'It's been a good day, most productive for us all.'

*

Daniel Rogers was another relation of ours. He would have been with them at Mortlake had he not been in Antwerp on business at the time.

His maternal grandmother was our father's sister, so his mother was Dutch but his father, John, was English. He and his siblings were born in Wittenberg in Germany when their father, a preacher, was stationed there. They went back to England to live. There, his father, John Rogers, became the first martyr when Mary, the Catholic queen, reigned in England, before Queen Elizabeth's time. He was burnt at the stake for being Protestant. Daniel was fifteen at the time.

'I didn't know whether to be proud or absolutely horrified. Mother kept us children home that day to prevent us seeing the gory details,' he explained. 'There's a fine line between the futility of martyrdom and the value of the witness about faith that it gives to others. I'm not sure on which side of that line I sit.'

After Daniel's father had been martyred, Abraham sold John's library at the Frankfurt Book Fair and sent the proceeds to Daniel's family.

While Rogers was still young, he had lived in Paris for a while acting as steward and teacher for Sir Henry Norris, a friend of John Dee. After an education at Oxford University, he acquired suitable talents, credentials and introductions to be able to take up the position of clerk of the

Council of Queen Elizabeth. The Queen often employed Rogers as personal envoy to the Netherlands and other parts. He acted with diligence and caution at all times and the Queen's Council benefitted from information that he collected about proceedings of foreign governments. Was he perhaps a spy?

Rogers was affiliated at this time to the Church of England. *Protestantissimus*, as Abe said. He was a close friend of William Camden, and also interested in maps. They were essential tools for a spy. In those times, many a traitorous spy worked for a foreign enemy, producing maps of his own country, for a price, of course, so that the enemy could successfully invade his home land. Rogers didn't go as far as that.

Abraham had sent Rogers a copy of the *Theatrum*. In return, Rogers sent Abraham a map of Ireland that he thought would be a great addition to the *Theatrum*. It was included in a later edition. Rogers had written a description to go with it in complicated elegiac verse, for he occasionally liked to write poetry. He had also written a book about the manners, laws and customs of the ancient Britons. William Camden had done likewise in his *Britannia*. In the 1578 and later editions of the *Theatrum*, Abraham inserted into the introductory pages a witticism in Latin verse that Rogers had sent him. So Rogers wrote him a letter in which he complimented him on the glory he would reap from posterity by his geographical works. Rogers mentioned his own commentary upon the laws and customs of the ancient Britons, just in case Abraham would be interested.

And Rogers gave Abraham some advice about beginning an *album amicorum*. 'Don't lock your friends in your heart alone. Writing is more faithful,' he said.

*

1577 was the year that Philip Galle engraved and coloured a becoming portrait of Abraham. He had copied it from a recent painting by Antonio Moro. It was a special gift for Abe's fiftieth birthday: an occasion marked with celebrations in England and later in Antwerp.

The portrait showed him looking very serious, dressed in his embroidered purple doublet, his vest of fur and his finest neck ruffle. His thinning hair and neatly sculptured beard were rather eye-catching. He was tall and had an easy stance, but that can't be captured in a bust portrait.

The portrait was enclosed in a locket design, at the top of which was a roundel depicting entwined Greek letters chi and rho, the sign for Christ, with alpha and omega signifying that Christ was the beginning and end of all things. For Galle knew that Abraham was a deeply religious man at heart. Which religion, one could never be sure, but surely a Christian of sorts. Beyond the roundel was a decorative background. The decorations of flora and foliage represented Abraham's interest in the natural world and were quite striking. At the bottom, Galle added a memorial line for him: 'Ortelius gave mortals the world to look at, and Galle gave the world Ortelius to look at.'

From then on, Abraham included that portrait in the *Theatrum*.

'Might as well let the world know what you look like,' I said.

21

When we returned from England, things still hadn't settled down in Antwerp after the Spanish Fury. So Abraham decided to do some more travelling, this time south to Italy. Joris Hoefnagel went with him. They left again in autumn, as that was the best time of the year for travelling before the cold winter set in. But the cold of the south was much milder than at home. The pair of them could never see enough of Italy, both in its present loveliness as well as its signs of ancient Roman civilisation. It was also a good time to be out of Antwerp. Abraham didn't like political unrest of any kind.

I was eager to hear of their adventures when they got home again.

On the way, they stopped at Augsburg in Germany. Our Ortels ancestors had lived there from time immemorial. Situated on a high plateau and surrounded by a rim of hills resembling a cooking basin, Augsburg was a large city on a major trading route.

Abraham described how they had inspected three old and ornate fountains which continuously spouted water into adjoining pools. The interior of the Golden Hall was decorated with gold filigree. They marvelled at such opulence.

'We visited relatives who lived in the centre of the city and looked to see if our grandfather William's house was still standing. It was, but it was beginning to look run-down, a bit like a decrepit old lady. A far cry from the huge Fugger house where we stayed as guests of Markus and Hans Fugger of the famous and influential banking family. The Fuggers had become very wealthy through banking, trading and mining, but to their credit they put some of their money into building houses for the poor to rent for next to nothing.'

Abraham and Hoefnagel had hoped to inspect Hans's enormous library of twelve thousand books and his collection of prints and antiquities.

'I was particularly interested in his set of drawings of ancient coins,' he said. 'And to round off a perfect day, we were treated to a sumptuous Fugger meal of mushroom soup followed by roast capons and rabbit. Little marzipan fruits and a red wine finished it off perfectly.'

Abe told me that Duke Albert of Bavaria was also there at dinner that night. He spoke with Hoefnagel about his art, praising his miniatures of plants and insects.

'If you'd be willing, I'd like to hire you as court artist,' invited the duke.

'You do me a great honour, sir. I'd be most pleased to accept your invitation.' Abe was pleased for him too.

A humanist friend, Markus Welser, also lived in Augsburg, where he was a politician of some rank. Abraham had corresponded with him frequently through their mutual interest in numismatics and ancient cartography. So Abraham and Hoefnagel visited him and spent a stimulating evening pouring over his enormous coin collection.

It was in this city that the Peace of Augsburg had been negotiated in 1555, a peace in which religious tolerance between Lutherans and Catholics was established.

'It's a pity such a situation couldn't be brought about in Antwerp,' said Abraham. 'Augsburg even has an annual holiday in August to celebrate the peace.'

Then it was over the Alps, bumping along on the back of an ox cart with a party of merchants, and into Italy. While they were wandering around Italy on foot or on donkeys, Hoefnagel painted pictures of cities and important country towns to include in the continuing volumes of *Civitates orbis terrarum*. Every so often, he incorporated in a corner in minute detail the pair of them trudging along on a dusty road or scanning the landscape before them.

It was a pleasant trip of several months. Early in the journey, the countryside was picturesque in its crimson and golden shades of autumn. The vines were being pruned, having lost all their leaves, and the corn stood high. Later, as it got colder and wetter, the countryside wore a grassy mantle. It's no wonder Hoefnagel had as his motto, 'Nature is the only teacher.'

They went as far south as Naples before boarding a ship that took them to Marseille, from where they snaked home again up the rivers.

22

1582 was the year the calendar changed. Ten days were lost in that year as 5 October became 15 October. Pfft! Gone! Just like that! It was bad enough that each year seemed to pass at a greater rate than the last, let alone ten days being completely removed.

And the beginning of the year changed from March to January.

Pope Gregory made the changes to guarantee the correct length of the solar year down to the last second, and to make sure that Easter was celebrated on the proper date as it had been in the fourth century. All a bit confusing, really!

23

We Dutch had suffered the Spanish Fury in 1576, then seven years later the French Fury was thrust upon us. The French Fury was an attempt by Francis, Duke of Anjou, to conquer the city of Antwerp. It failed. Anjou, who was both brother of the French king and heir to the French throne, had been approached by William of Orange to rule over the Seventeen Provinces of the Netherlands, to get the support of the French in expelling the Spanish troops. The pasty-faced Anjou didn't have much influence in the Netherlands and attempted to seize more power. He tried to occupy Antwerp by surprise. Unfortunately for Anjou, his plan was discovered.

On 17 January 1583, in an attempt to fool the citizens of Antwerp, Anjou had asked to be permitted to enter the city in order to honour its people with a royal entry. As soon as Anjou's troops entered the city, the gates of Antwerp were slammed shut behind them. The small French army found itself hopelessly trapped within the city.

Our people bombarded them from windows and rooftops with stones, rocks, chunks of firewood and even heavy chains: anything they could lay their hands on. The city's garrison then opened point-blank fire on the troops. Only a few Frenchmen, including the Duke of Anjou himself, escaped. Over fifteen hundred troops perished, many of them hacked to death by the enraged citizens of Antwerp. The inhabitants, still traumatised by the plunder of the Spanish Fury, were determined to prevent another occupation by foreign troops by all means possible.

Abraham had no part in this slaughter. In fact, he hardly poked his head out the door while it was all going on.

The position of Anjou in the Netherlands after this attack became untenable and he slunk out of our country for good, like a rat that had managed to escape a trap.

24

Relations with the Spanish deteriorated. There was another uprising in 1584 when King Philip's Spanish army invaded again. On his march towards us, he captured town after town, city after city. Ypres, Ghent, Bruges and Brussels, all had rebelled against his violence and religious intolerance. The Spanish soldiers led by the Duke of Parma seemed invincible. Antwerp was the only city left in Dutch hands. It was heavily fortified with a modern artillery fortress and big guns.

The defence of Antwerp was headed by our burgomeister. Dutch rebels broke the dykes and flooded the countryside to isolate the Spanish army on islands of higher ground hoping to cut off their supplies. However, Parma was smarter than that. He cut off all the supply routes to Antwerp and blockaded the city in order to starve its people out of existence. For months, it went on and on.

Parma built a bridge of boats across the River Scheldt. Dutch soldiers sent unmanned fire ships loaded with explosives into the bridge, trying to break the blockade. Then one fire ship destroyed all the boats. The explosion killed eight hundred Spaniards but Parma escaped by the skin of his teeth. Although a breakthrough, the Dutch were unable to complete the work.

In May 1585, our troops made a final attempt to break the blockade by a two-pronged attack on a Spanish-held fort on the main dyke. Fighting was heavy. The burgomeister, thinking that Antwerp had already won, sailed to the city to announce the victory. But Parma rekindled the fighting spirit of his soldiers and it wasn't long before they'd rallied and won the battle. The attempt to break the blockade had failed and Antwerp's situation was now desperate. We were tired of fighting, and hungry as our food supplies ran out.

We were actually starving after living on next to nothing for fourteen months. No roast fowl, no poached fish, no juicy red apples crossed our lips. Even flour for bread was running out. We were left with a few old and withered root vegetables from our cellars and the odd egg that our hungry hens had laid. Our soup was watery with very little substance.

And we were tired too, for often the sound of cannon fire extended into the night. No sleep after days of being worried and terrified. Abraham tried to make himself scarce in these months, but there was no way he could escape the city this time. He wouldn't admit to being afraid and distressed but I know he was. He sat in his comfortable chair in front of the open fire reading books, learning something new all the time, while I sat beside him spinning greasy fleeces. Abraham thought about Cicero again, about his saying, 'There's no place more delightful than one's own fireplace.'

'Even in the midst of troubles, that wisdom is true,' Abraham said. 'What's the point of worrying anyway? It gets you nowhere.' It simply wasn't his style to go out and get involved in the fray.

*

Three months later, when Antwerp surrendered to the Duke of Parma and his Spanish troops, Parma marched his soldiers in through the gate in the city walls and stationed them within Antwerp to prevent rioting. He issued strict instructions not to completely sack the city. The troops were surprisingly disciplined and honourable. Not a single incident was reported.

Frans Hogenberg made an engraving showing the entry of the Duke of Parma's troops into Antwerp. He showed them passing in an orderly way over the moat, through the city gate and marching up the street to the centre of the city. The horsemen with their long pikes were led by two soldiers blowing their shawms.

Parma decreed that all Protestants had to leave the city within two years: he gave them a time of grace to settle their affairs. We stayed.

When the city surrendered and fell under control of the Spaniards, it was the beginning of the end for the Netherlands as we knew it. The north and the south were divided. The north remained in the hands of the Dutch rebels, while the south stayed under control of the Spanish.

More than half the population fled the city, including many skilled artists and tradesmen, teachers and leaders of commerce. Many went to Amsterdam, for they feared a repeat of former atrocities. Antwerp became but a shadow of its former self. No wonder they called the whole incident the Fall of Antwerp.

25

During and just after the Fall of Antwerp in 1585, our cousin, Joachim Ortels, was acting as a go-between the Dutch and the English.

He was a facts man. Born in Augsburg in Germany in 1542, he emigrated first to Antwerp and then later to London. He worked ostensibly as a silk merchant. He was appointed Dutch agent to the English queen in 1583. While deeply involved at a leadership level with the Dutch Church at Austin Friars in London, he lived near the van Meteren and Colius families, who were all his relatives.

It is really quite irrelevant that he was related to us in some obscure way; they had the same surname after all. But like us he was a Dutchman through and through, even though he had lived in London for a long time. He spoke English with no trace of an accent and was familiar with English culture and habits.

At about this time, he was negotiating on behalf of the Dutch with the queen of England, through one of her top advisors. In a desperate attempt to defeat the Spanish and hold off their occupation, the Dutch had offered the Netherlands' crown to both the queen of England and the king of France. Both refused the offer, even though they were sworn enemies of Philip II of Spain. Queen Elizabeth said that she didn't want power over the Netherlands, only to preserve the freedom of our people.

Nevertheless, to ease her conscience, Queen Elizabeth promised to send some troops; not very many, though: just a token amount. But she dilly-dallied around so much about how many she'd send and who would lead them that they arrived too late to intervene in the siege that led to the Fall of Antwerp.

Three days after the Fall, she drew up the Treaty of Nonsuch. By its terms, she promised to protect the Netherlands and immediately give an annual subsidy of 600,000 florins. However, it didn't come cheaply. Our ports of Flushing and Brill were to pass into English hands.

*

It was Abraham's friendship with the poet, Peter Heyns, that got him into strife at this time.

Immediately after the Fall of Antwerp, Heyns had fled to Germany and then went to the northern part of the Netherlands. He was a strongly opinionated and loudly voiced Calvinist who sympathised with the Dutch revolutionaries. This had worked against him a couple of times before; he too had escaped to England in 1577 when we did.

Because of their friendship, the Spanish thought Abraham might be as much of a troublemaker as Heyns. Abe was investigated and arrested. The Spanish left him in a dark and damp cellar for three days before they questioned him with intent. Abraham wasn't particularly disconcerted about being in the dark for so long, but he was intimidated by the aggressive interrogation. However, when they learnt who he was, they let him go.

'So I too was not trusted by the Spanish and Catholic authorities,' Abraham said. 'It took me a long time to convince them that I was in truth a good Catholic, and to regain my civic rights. I even tried to bribe members of the higher ranks by giving them maps in order to be accepted again.'

But what they didn't know was that while on the surface Abraham's relationship with Heyns seemed no more than an ordinary friendship between people who saw a lot of each other, there was more. I too was involved. I lent Heyns a considerable amount of money; I had to secure a loan on some of our houses to do this. I could do so because of my share of the family inheritance and the fact that not being married gave me financial rights that other women handed over to their husbands.

It was a worrying time.

*

Although our nephew Jacob Colius was born in Antwerp, he had lived in London all his life. While he'd been writing letters to Abraham since he first learnt to write, now that things had quietened down in Antwerp after the great Fall of 1585, he was able to come back to Antwerp and stay with us. He was in his twenties by then. It was good for him to be with Abraham, they shared so many interests.

'I remember that trip well, Uncle,' he said later. 'While I was there, I learnt a lot, including some of the finer skills of gardening. You managed to grow such a lot of handsome flowers and fresh herbs and vegetables in your little backyard. I think Cicero might have been largely correct when he said, "If you have a garden and a library, you have everything you need."'

He chuckled, then went on. 'Thanks, Aunt Ann, for the valerian and sunflower seeds that you sent from your garden. They have grown well in London.'

'I know you wanted some African marigold seeds as well, but none of my contacts could get hold of any for you,' Abraham responded.

'We did a lot of walking too,' continued Jacob, 'in the park examining what grew in the garden beds. And there, dabbling around the edge of the pond, was the most handsome little duck with curled-up wing tips and striking orange, white and purple markings. A mandarin duck, you said, that had originally come from countries of the Far East. I've never seen the likes of it. You know so much about everything, Uncle Abraham,' Jacob said fondly.

And while he was in Antwerp, Jacob immersed himself in Abraham's huge library. 'Thanks for sending a letter to my father telling him that you'd observed with pleasure that I was reading and learning every day,' he said. 'He's insistent that I keep on learning, just like you!'

Abraham was also pleased when Jacob reported that the *Civitates* book was selling well in London.

And Jacob was pleased to use Jacob Colius Ortelianus as his signature after this time.

26

Abraham never lost his interest in maps and map making. Until very late in life, he continued to seek out other cartographers and different kinds of maps. And of course he continued revising and adding to the collection that made up the *Theatrum*.

Apart from the modern maps in the mapbook, he compiled a series of historical maps known as the *Parergon theatri*. Making them was an extra activity that he delighted in over and above his ordinary maps.

The *Parergon* maps were at first separate publications but later he included them as supplements to the *Theatrum*. Four of them appeared at first in 1579; he added to their number from time to time, until there were more than forty. They were not based on editing of other people's work like the *Theatrum* maps, but rather were his own work. He'd put a lot of meticulous research and skill into producing them.

The maps illustrated ancient history. As well, Abraham inserted information from the classical authors like Strabo, Pliny and Herodotus; and the Bible too.

A map of the Roman Empire was one of the first of the *Parergon* maps. The accompanying text gave a history of Rome itself. It began in an impressive manner: 'At the time that triumphant Rome first began to grow to the credit and honour of the world, so that it might further rise by degrees and lofty increments to become a firm league of eternal peace, virtue and fortune...'

The oval cartouches in the top corners show a portrait of Romulus, the founder of the eternal city, and of the poet, Tibullus, who wrote, 'Rome, your race is destined to rule the world.' The lower cartouches contain a list of the origins and growth of the Roman Empire. The list definitely isn't short. It also shows a genealogy of the seven kings of

Rome. A diagram of the family tree of the founders of Rome – Romulus and Remus – is included. Legends about different family members are superimposed upon the tree. It is a crowded map of elegant design as well as an accurate depiction of Europe as it was in Roman times. Abraham was proud of it.

Another early *Parergon* map is of the travels of St Paul, using information from the Acts of the Apostles in the Bible. It has two oval-shaped painted medallions in the top portion. One is of the conversion of Saul on his way to Damascus, not in the Italian Alps as Bruegel had depicted. The other shows Paul being shipwrecked on the coast of Malta. Saul and Paul were his names before and after his conversion.

It was Abraham's friends who persuaded him to include these maps of the ancient world as a supplement to the *Theatrum*.

*

I was particularly taken with a map of his namesake in the *Parergon*. I thought that Mother would be absolutely delighted looking down from up there in heaven. It was in 1590 that this map first appeared in the *Theatrum*.

The map, 'The wanderings and life of the patriarch Abraham', has small painted medallions around the edge telling Abraham's story. A banner along the top and bottom of the map itself has the Biblical version of the story: 'Abraham, you must depart from your land, and leave your relatives, and come to the land that I will show you; and I will give you and your offspring the land of Canaan to be yours forever.'

An inset map shows the road actually taken by Abraham, all calculated from the Bible story. Immediately below, the text states that the privilege Ortelius has on the map is for a ten-year period. And in the cartouche on the right is the dedication, 'To my friend, the noble lord Joannes Moflinius, a respected clergyman and chaplain to the King of Spain.' Abe had visited him at Luxembourg on their 1575 journey to those parts.

But what I particularly liked were the twenty-two small medallions

155

around the edge that showed delightful pictures of the biblical Abraham's life. Our friend, Martin de Vos, drew them and I enjoyed colouring them. If you begin at the top and proceed in a clockwise direction, you can follow the story of Abraham from the call of Abraham and his people to leave his city, to his burial in a cave.

*

Martin de Vos liked to boast about the medallions that he drew for the map of the wanderings of Abraham.

'Twenty-two of them there were,' he bragged, 'tiny vignettes arranged around the edge of the map of Palestine. Delicate little miniatures depicting the life and wanderings of Abraham from his departure from Ur until his death.'

There is a huge amount of detail in both the foreground and the background of the tiny 17.5-*duimen* circles.

'You can see smoke rising from a fire on the altar in one of them and a family dog in the foreground of another,' de Vos pointed out. 'They took me a long time to draw with very fine brushes. When they were complete they were engraved onto the copper printing plates before you coloured them, Ann. I have to confess to using another artist's works on a similar theme as inspiration for these drawings,' de Vos said, 'but I added my own touch to them too.'

The full story is in the Book of Genesis in the Bible.

*

Lucas Waghenaer found maps irresistible too, and marine charts. He was bound to cross Abe's path at some point, and Abe was bound to tell me about him.

'Waghenaer is an experienced seaman and pilot. For thirty years, he has sailed the high seas. He has met and consulted with Portuguese, Spanish and Italian seafarers about the safest routes for his ships. He has produced his own navigational charts for many years, but it was quite some time before he published a collection for use by others. His knowledge of maritime charts and sailing instructions that he'd gained from foreign contacts are the foundation of his maps. He put a lot of energy into making them and consulted my maps for ideas on presentation. So they came out looking quite splendid with the same sorts of fancy cartouches, ships in full sail and monstrous fish that are so common on maps today.'

'A map would be quite boring without those illustrations,' I said.

'But more than that, his nautical charts and sailing directions contain all the latest knowledge of navigation and position-finding. They are sure to set a standard for years to come. *The mariners' mirror*, as he calls his collection, covers coastlines from Holland to Spain, and from the Baltic to the North Sea. Only coastal place names are given. They are important locations for fixing position. Cliffs on the coastline are drawn in elevation. Navigational landmarks and hazards, anchorages, soundings and tidal details are shown. And the scale is in English, Spanish and Dutch measures. They were quite different from ordinary maps like I produced. Christopher Plantin printed them for him. They are well liked, with several reprints necessary to meet demand. They have even been printed in England. In fact, they are so popular there that people call them Waggoners, a term which quickly came to mean any sea charts.'

So Abraham went to see him, hoping to obtain some of the charts. Later, he congratulated Plantin on producing a first in the history of maritime cartography.

*

In his old age, Abraham was still producing new maps. In 1589, he published *Maris Pacifici*. He was sure that it was the first map of just the Pacific Ocean to be printed. It was also the first to name North and South America separately. The land mass that lay to the south of the whole Pacific was called Terra Australis, the great South Land.

Abraham called the map 'A very new description of the peaceful sea, commonly called the South Sea, with the regions lying around it and its islands scattered everywhere'. Sometimes, his detailed titles are verbose.

The map is based on a recent map of America drawn by Frans Hogenberg who is usually remembered for his engraving rather than his drawing. However, he drew it as well this time, but on Abraham's instructions. It also strongly relied on a 1569 map of Mercator.

Abraham had used Spanish and Portuguese manuscripts to correct many misunderstandings about America. Quite a few of the new place names along the North American west coast were provided by Richard Hakluyt in his new book of recent explorations.

'Did you happen to notice that in the middle of the ocean is a huge Spanish galleon proudly riding the sea victoriously with flags flying, sails unfurled and guns shooting?' Abraham asked me. 'It's the *Victoria*. The text beneath the ship says it all: "I was the first to sail around the world and carried you, Magellan, leader, first through the straits. I sailed around the world, therefore I am justly called *Victory*. My sails were my wings, my prize was glory, my fight was with the sea." The Spanish have gone to great lengths to find and control any possible sea passage to the East Indies via South America.'

Abraham corrected previous maps to show that the huge island of New Guinea and the smaller islands of Japan were closer to Asia than America. He also adjusted the width of America so that it became quite narrow on the Tropic of Capricorn.

'This text block on the map contains a snippet of history,' said Abraham. 'In the region of China, as also in Japan and neighbouring isles, many were converted to the Christian faith by Jesuit priests. As you know, I have many good Jesuit friends.'

The text that Abraham wrote to accompany this map is a full geography and history lesson all in one: fascinating and novel.

Firstly, all the ancient names for the Pacific are recorded. Pliny called it Eoum. Ptolemy incorrectly called it *Sinus Magnus*, the Great Bay, whereas he should have called it *Mare Magnum*, the Great Sea. Marco

Polo called it *Mare Cin*, the Smokey Sea. It was discovered only a lifetime ago by Ferdinand Magellan of Portugal, who greeted it in the year 1520.

Next is an account of Magellan's voyage, including a record of his death in 1521 in the Philippines.

Abraham notes that there are more than seven thousand islands in the Pacific. In some parts, weeds rise out of the water, giving the impression of not sailing through the sea but rather through a green meadow or a pleasant grove.

Then he speculates on the loss of Magellan's ship, *Victoria*. What became of it, who knows? In antiquity, they would have claimed that it went up into the skies, like the mythological ship the *Argo*.

Plato had claimed that the sea around the island of Atlantis was unnavigable because of slime remaining after most of the island had sunk into the ocean. Fanciful stories indeed, but Abraham likes to add a classical dimension wherever he can.

After a tribute to Christopher Columbus, Abraham describes the lands that surround the sea and the peoples who live there. He writes that Estotiland abounds with all that is necessary for human life. Estotiland is that part of America which lies closest to Greenland, Iceland and Friesland. In the middle of Estotiland stands a high mountain from which four rivers spring that provide water to the whole country. The inhabitants are intelligent and skilled in all kinds of handicrafts. They use their own language and alphabet. They say that in their king's library there are even some books in Latin, which they can't understand.'

'How did they get there,' I asked.

'They may have been left by some Christian missionaries who were in contact with them,' replied Abraham. 'There seems to be all kinds of metal there, but especially lots of gold. They trade with the people of Greenland, from whom they obtain hides, tar and brimstone.'

'It seems that the people of Estotiland are almost civilised,' I said.

Abraham also points out that nearer to the North Pole is another large country, another new world. Its inhabitants are barbarous and go about naked. They protect themselves against the winter cold with animal skins. They don't use metal. In fact, they know nothing of it, but live by hunting. For weapons, they use long spears and arrows, especially in war with one another. They obey governors and laws.

And on the coast of Peru, shells can be found that yield pearls, precious pearls of the finest nacre. Mother liked pearls!

*

'It was a bit of joke really,' confessed Johannes Wacker when he met us us over a beer. 'A map of a hypothetical place.'

Thomas More, who had his head removed by Henry VIII, had written a book called *Utopia* about an ideal imaginary island and its political system. Wacker suggested that Abraham might like to make a map of the place as an illustration for copies of the book. Abraham chuckled and said he couldn't be bothered, but eventually he reluctantly did so.

'What a lark!' said Wacker. He was a bit of a joker, always trying to get people to laugh.

Abraham wrote in a cartouche on the map, 'Behold the happy kingdom. This is Utopia, bulwark of peace, centre of love and justice, best harbour and good shore. It offers a happy life.'

Wacker contributed all the names on this map; many were after the style of More himself. Most were nonsense, and often the same name occurred but in many different languages, so that each nation might recognise something of itself in all this. The four regions on the mainland that lay north of the island of Utopia were inhabited by People without land, Windy people, Lucky people and Mercenaries.

Among the rivers, names can be found that translate to River without water, River without a riverbed, Non-flowing river, River without fish, River without boats, River out of a jug.

Wacker also provided a list of town names for the map. And again, more peculiar names appeared: City that never existed, City without life, City without houses, City of the happy thigh bone and Swamp of the foolish. What an imagination!

Abraham dedicated the map to Johannes Mattheus Wacker von Wackerfels, giving him his full title, and added the invitation, 'Enjoy and be well!'

Actually, he was rather embarrassed by the whole thing. He never put it into any edition of the *Theatrum*. It almost made a mockery of More's book. It didn't sell very well either.

*

It wasn't until 1598 that Mercator's complete *Atlas* was finally finished. Years and years of painstaking work. It consisted of six volumes which were each published as they were finished, between 1578 and 1598. Mercator had died in 1594 so it was his son who completed the atlas after his death.

Unlike Abraham, who mostly edited maps that he obtained from various sources, Mercator redrew all of his from scratch. He was a perfectionist. As he grew older, he found travelling tiresome, so obtained most of his maps through lengthy correspondences. While Abraham's mapbook proved to be immensely popular and ran to many editions, Mercator hoped that his, based on scientific principles and with only a minimum of ornamental aspects, would be significant for centuries to come.

27

In the time that followed the *Theatrum,* Abraham not only continued to produce historical maps for the *Parergon* collection, but also some small books on other classical interests.

Over the years, he built up a fine collection of coins, medals and antiquities which he described and illustrated in a book with a long Latin name, *Deorum dearumque capita...,* The heads of gods and goddesses... It was illustrated with ten engravings done by Philip Galle, who also published it, in 1573. Abraham included illustrations of coins on some of his *Parergon* maps too.

As a complement to the historical maps of the *Parergon,* Abraham produced in 1579 an alphabetical list of ancient place names, including their modern names in Latin and Dutch. Peoples, regions, islands, towns, mountains, forests, lakes, rivers, all were inserted in this *Nomenclator Ptolemaicus.* The names were referenced from the works of Ptolemy. At first, this was attached as an appendix to the *Theatrum,* but later a few copies were bound separately. It turned out to be a most popular production. As always, updates appeared continuously.

I myself could never understand why people liked lists and more lists.

Earlier, in 1578, Plantin had published Abraham's *Synonymia geographica,* a similar project listing place names, but this time it was all the place names known to Abraham. This project was neither new nor his own idea. Many others had tried what Abraham and his old friend Arnold Mylius strove for in this work. Mylius had been building and organising a card index for many years, ever since Abraham had started working on the *Theatrum.* The names were gathered from literary and historical sources, including the Bible and old coins, as well as contemporary authorities. Abraham particularly noted some references to old names for the New World of America: *Atlantis Insula, Oceanus Atlanticus* and *Ophir*.

Nine years later, the *Synonymia* was republished with a new name, *Thesaurus Geographicus*, and later again in 1596 an expanded edition appeared that had thirty thousand names in it. A veritable treasury of names.

There were no maps in any of the *Nomenclator, Synonymia* or *Thesaurus*.

In the text of the 1596 edition of the *Thesaurus*, Abraham introduced an entirely novel concept. Looking carefully at a map of the world and considering the coasts of three continents, he could see that the Americas might have been torn away from Europe and Africa by earthquakes and floods.

'The vestiges of the rupture reveal themselves,' he said. 'It is as if the American continent had drifted away from the African and European continents!'

I hope that's not a heretical statement!

Other works of Abraham's later years were *Caesaris omnia quae extant*, which was published in 1593, and *Aurei saeculi imago, sive Germanorum veterum vita, mores, ritus et religio iconibus delineate*, which came out in 1596. They became known as *Caesaris* and *Aurei* for short.

The former was about what was known of Caesar from still existing sources. Raphelingen, married to one of Plantin's daughters, published it for Abraham, for Plantin had died in 1589. Christopher's death hit Abe hard.

The latter, *Aurei*, was a short commentary on the life, manners, customs, rites and religion of the ancient Germans, inspired by golden coins of the time. It included such subjects as childhood and family life. For this book, Abraham had gathered together the works of ancient writers on Germany. He illustrated it with ten engravings. Philip Galle published it for him.

28

Over the years, as always, Abraham kept in touch with humanist friends, even though the original circle had diminished as people passed on. But new ones were always coming along to take their places.

One of them was Justus Lipsius. Abraham called him the young pup, for he was twenty years his junior. His curly hair and direct gaze reminded me of a young poodle sometimes, soft at heart, but determined and not willing to let go of the bone.

Lipsius was well-known as an intellectual, knowledgeable in many fields. He told us that he began his studies as a novice in the Jesuit College of Cologne, where he was considered a prodigy with an extraordinary memory. Then he spent a couple of years in Rome in his early twenties, serving as secretary to Cardinal de Granvelle, who worked for Philip II of Spain. There, he had the opportunity to visit many great libraries and to work with the best of the Italian humanists.

'Later, I taught at the Catholic university of Leuven,' Lipsius explained, 'followed by the Lutheran university of Jena in Germany and then the new University of Leiden, which was overrun by Calvinists. Of course, among all those different religions, I had to belong to the right one each time. Easy when you believe that the variety doesn't matter, it's the Christianity at the heart that is important.'

His passion was for the writings of the ancients, particularly Tacitus and Seneca. As a linguist, he studied ancient written records in order to work out how authentic they were and what they meant.

Lipsius's chief contribution to our times was the revival of Stoicism, the Greek philosophy of hanging in there in bad times. In 1582, his *On constancy* was published, putting the case that a life of steadfast virtue was its own reward, regardless of circumstances and misfortunes.

'My neo-Stoicism emphasised three responses to our turbulent times: personal discipline, an ethical lifestyle and rational judgement. And so I taught people to use reflection on their lives as a basis for action, particularly for those in high places,' he said.

He also produced a work with the title *Six books of politics*. 'I gathered together sayings from the ancients and created a collection of political guidelines to be used by monarchs to control their kingdoms. However, I'm not optimistic that these principles might be put into practice quickly, if at all.'

He held the opinion that ideal citizens were people who acted according to reason, were answerable to themselves, in control of their emotions and ready to fight. Such notions found wide acceptance in our troubled times. When translated to politics, this view called for a thorough reorganisation of the state and its government. Such a reorganisation would include rule by royalty not by conquerors, justice for subjects and the disciplinary measures to achieve it, and a strong military defence.

He also put together a treatise on the Roman military which he hoped would inspire some modern military reforms. He wanted an opportunity to advise King Philip II about a way to a peaceful settlement to the religious strife that wracked our country.

These principles caught on and became very popular. His works were sold, reprinted and translated across Europe.

'Of course, many of my ideas were honed in humanist discussions and continuing correspondence from you, Ortelius. I was obsessive about humanism.'

Abraham admired him a lot.

*

Dirck Coornhert continued to be an acquaintance of Abraham, even though they didn't always agree about matters.

On several occasions, Cornhert had reason to criticise Abraham for not speaking out for what he believed about religious freedom when it mattered, for escaping to other countries in times of religious troubles and, in general, for being passive. As I've said before, Abraham hated dissension of any kind, most of all fighting and war. He wasn't alone in that.

'Hiding away from it all doesn't further anyone's cause,' Coornhert accused. 'You ought to stand up and be counted.'

29

Our home, de Vlasbloem, the Flax Flower, near the hospital, was too small to hold all of Abe's collections. There wasn't much room to move between piles of unopened boxes. We had to shift into something bigger to fit them all in. We bought a step-gabled house called the Rode leeuw, the Red Lion, in the Rue du Convent and enlarged it by buying the house next door, the Laurel Tree. These were in addition to the small Flax Flower, where we continued to live.

So Abraham established a museum to show off all his precious things. Actually, it was me who arranged and catalogued it all, under Abraham's expert direction of course. But he left the finer details to me.

Several rooms, his library, were full of books. He liked what Cicero had to say about libraries: 'A room without books is like a body without a soul.' The front rooms held all his antiquities and curiosities.

As a matter of fact, I quite liked the weekly cleaning of them all, even though it took forever. Each of the hundreds of books had to be taken off the shelf and both the book and the shelf wiped with a cloth. And each specimen had to be picked up and wiped separately and carefully.

In this museum, ancient artefacts like Roman and Greek statues, inscriptions, medallions and coins of gold, silver and copper could be found, along with many natural objects of great beauty and rarity like his pieces of marble of all colours from distant parts of the world and some large shells from India. They also all needed wiping carefully at least once a week. I liked to stroke the white marble bust of Julius Caesar and a smooth and delicate pink shell that had spider-like appendages. Abraham had some mottled tortoiseshell tabletops of various sizes, one so large that ten people could comfortably sit around it. That must have been one giant tortoise.

In the corner, I placed a carved wooden curiosity cabinet with its legs of sculpted animal heads. Its many drawers each had a pretty miniature scene painted on the front. I carefully arranged smaller things in the drawers. Popular with visitors were many and varied little shells, a pair of iridescent scarab beetles, some sea urchins and a stuffed hummingbird, along with gems given to him by wealthy admirers from abroad. I was quite nervous about the possibility of dropping a set of opalescent bird's eggs.

Pride of place was given to a small and ancient Chinese terracotta statue of a horse's head that was presented to Abraham by a Jesuit missionary friend. Almost completely covering the walls were paintings and prints that he had acquired over the years.

Abe particularly valued an ancient Greek tetradrach, a coin with a beady-eyed owl perched on it. I guess he was fond of it because Athena's owl represented peace in the land. He often wondered whether we would ever achieve peace in our land.

Many visitors, both locals and foreigners, came to visit the *Museum Ortelianum*. Some people came to check things out for reference purposes, others just to gaze upon beautiful objects.

While I showed people around the museum, I liked to wear my carved tortoiseshell comb in my silvering hair, and the pearl earrings that Abraham gave me for my sixtieth birthday.

The museum came to be a magnet in the city.

30

Abraham greatly appreciated the drawings for the *Civitates* and the paintings that Joris Hoefnagel had done. One day, unexpectedly, Hoefnagel presented Abraham with a painting that he'd made of him. It was not actually a painting of him but about him. Did it show him as tall and handsome with a receding hairline? No, it was an allegorical painting that told much more about who he was in Joris's eyes than what he looked like.

Known as *Hermathena,* its central figure was an owl sitting on a globe that rested on a large book. The owl represented the mythical figure of Athena with her quality of peace. The globe outlined the countries of Europe, Africa and the Near East; it sprouted olive branches, the olive branches of peace. The book was the mapbook, the *Theatrum.* The owl had one talon on the globe and the other held a small staff of the kind that Roman officers carried to signify that they had come in peace. The staff brought to mind Hermes, that mythical figure of wisdom who always had one at his side. On closer inspection, it could be seen that the staff was actually a paintbrush. Further paintbrushes, a paint mixing pot, a compass and a stylus lay around the *Theatrum,* along with shells. The shells symbolised a soul that yearned for artistic creation and scientific discovery. The journey of the soul was also represented by a larva, a caterpillar and butterflies. A dragonfly that could seize its victims when it willed, signified death. The whole painting was in muted tones of the palest grey, vibrant brown and the lightest of tans: the colours of harmony and peace. It was a wonder.

So the picture showed Abraham to be a man of wisdom and peace who lived for the arts, the sciences and his spiritual faith; a man for whom peace held the answers to the world's conflicts. How we all wished it were so.

The picture also showed that Hoefnagel was a reflective and sensitive artist who saw beyond outward appearances to the depths of his friend.

'There is certainly something of you,' said Hoefnagel, 'in the transformation from the larva of promise of your youth, to the emerging caterpillar of a successful businessman, and finally to butterfly reality of the whole vibrant world of mapmaking.'

31

As was the custom among his circle of friends, Abraham kept an *album amicorum*, a book in which friends inscribed a complimentary message, or drew a picture or added a quote from some famous ancient scholar. All sorts of people contributed to Abraham's album: young and old, Protestant and Catholic, and living all over Europe. The one thing that all had in common, though, was that they were all humanists. The album was a way of honouring the deep friendships that had been formed.

It was important not to let Spanish authorities get hold of one's *album amicorum*, for they were sure to read something subversive into its entries; with drastic consequences.

Emanuel van Meteren had sent Abraham's album around to friends who had already left Antwerp and lived elsewhere, to get them to give Abraham a message. His own message to Abraham was a heartfelt one about trust, for they were the greatest of friends, Emanuel and Abraham, from when they were young children growing up together in Antwerp.

During those turbulent times, families had been uprooted and fortunes overturned, and faith had wavered. No one ever knew when, or even if, they would see their friends again. They could be here one day but gone the next. So it was important to have messages of hope from valued friends.

When Abraham was getting old and feeble, he was still carrying on with his works to the best of his ability. As he wrote to his favourite nephew, 'I am well in spirits but only reasonably so in the body. It's been a long time since you came to visit me, and it's not for want of an invitation.'

Jacob's reply was that he was a busy man, dealing in silk and researching natural history. And for such a long time it really wasn't all that safe to be in Antwerp, especially for a Protestant as he was.

Eventually, he came from London to Antwerp to visit us, perhaps for the last time. He didn't stay long, just in case. He called while on a field trip exploring the plants and animals and birds of Europe with a friend.

While he was here, he made an index for Abraham's *album amicorum* to make it easier for Abraham to find a particular friend's entry. Most of his oldest and closest friends had died by then. That was the trouble with getting old and living for a long time: friends had passed on, leaving one grieving. First to go was Peter Bruegel, then Hieronymus Cock, Gillis Coppens van Diest, Hans Collaert, Frans Hogenberg, Dirck Coornhert and Christopher Plantin. They'd all gone. Even Gerard Mercator, who was probably his dearest friend. Abraham outlived them all. They all had entries in his album; there were more than a hundred and thirty of them.

I too put a small one on the back page. I just signed it AO. I drew and coloured a small map of a mythical country and filled its unknown interior with monkeys in palm trees.

Abraham liked to go back over them all remembering those people and reflecting on his life with them. It often brought tears to his eyes as he recalled them. Many, many very good friends. As Cicero said, 'The harvest of old age is the recollection of an abundance of blessings previously secured.'

Christopher Plantin had written in the album, 'Such a considerable span of time, I feel obliged to your virtue and desirable graces, that my heart may be related to yours in a literal manner with amiable bonds.'

Abraham's dear friend Peter Bruegel was only forty-four when he died. It seemed so tragic when someone of great talent died so early in their life. He passed away before he got a chance to say something about Abraham, so Abraham wrote a tribute to him, in his own book.

This is what he wrote.

Peter Bruegel was the most perfect painter of his age. No one, unless jealous or envious or ignorant of his art, could ever deny it. He was snatched away from us in the flower of his life. I cannot say whether I should attribute it to Death, who thought Bruegel was more advanced in age than he actually was, when he observed the distinguished skill of his art, or whether I should attribute it to Nature, who feared that she would be held in contempt because of his artistic and talented skills at imitation. A grieving Abraham Ortelius consecrates this to the memory of his friend. When asked which of his predecessors he followed, the ancient Greek painter Eupompos comes to mind. He is said to have declared that he followed nature herself and he was not an artist. So with our Bruegel, whose pictures I would not really call *artificiosae*, but rather natural. Indeed, I would not call him the best of painters, but rather the very nature of painters. So I think that he is worthy of being followed by all. In all his works, more is always to be understood than he actually painted. Painters who paint pretty young people and wish to add some charm and grace of their own completely destroy the image presented to them, and stray both from the exemplar set before them and from true form. From this fault, our Bruegel was free.

While Jacob Colius was in Antwerp, Abraham invited him to offer an entry too. From when he was quite young, he had shared an interest in old coins with Abe. So in Abraham's album, Jacob sketched an ornament that Abraham had designed for the book on his numismatic collection, *Deorum dearumque...* The ornament represented the theme of honour. Then onto this ornament he drew a small picture of a tower on which God's name was written in Hebrew, and around the tower he inscribed in Latin, 'Refuge of the just', a reference to chapter 18 of the biblical book of Proverbs. It was a meaningful piece, and he signed it Jacob Cools Ortelianus, just to remind Abraham that he was his dearest uncle. In fact, Abraham quite approved, for he looked on Jacob more as a son than a nephew.

32

Abraham couldn't resist work on the *Peutinger Table*. It was a medieval copy of a fourth-century Roman road map of the routes that Roman soldiers passed along. The copy was of a map originally inscribed on marble in Imperial Rome in early AD. The medieval copy was found a century ago in a library in Augsburg and came into the hands of Konrad Peutinger who eventually passed it on to Markus Welser as he was unable to publish it himself.

Welser was captivated by its rarity and beauty. He had shared this find with Abraham much earlier. The *Peutinger Table* consisted of a series of eight elongated and adjacent road maps on four sheets. The map began in Spain and progressed eastward to the end of the known world, beyond Ceylon and India. In India, the map even showed the places where scorpions and elephants were born. It was a different concept of a map than previously known. Although the map showed towns, rivers and mountain ranges, and about 125,000 *mijls* of roads, it was not an accurate or real rendering of the landscape. The shapes of countries were not shown, it didn't attempt to show distances at the same scale, nor was north always at the top of the map.

Of course, Abraham was extremely excited to see it. 'Publish it,' he said. 'I'll help you with it. Just say what is needed and consider it done.'

But it took Welser many years to get around to publishing it. And then Abraham, the perfectionist when it came to maps, wasn't happy with the proof copy.

'Inadequate!' was his response. He thought that Welser was somewhat taken aback by that remark because his rejoinder was, 'Well, I suggest you make new copies yourself.'

So Abraham did, and he supervised the engraving of them, despite the aches and pains of his advancing age. However, he had left it too late to get it published; it wasn't printed before he died.

33

Abraham was slumped in his chair with a blanket falling off his knees. He sat beside the fire watching the flames dancing low among the glowing coals and occasionally let out a long despondent moan. His brow was burning with heat not from the fire but from within himself. He ached all over. Suddenly, a hacking cough sent another shot of stabbing pain into his chest. He doubled over and called me. 'Come and stay with me, please, Ann. I'm not sure I can take much more of this.'

'You poor dear. I'll get you some more laudanum, that should relieve the pain for a while at least.'

'Don't bother. It's horrible bitter stuff and I can do without it.' He took a deep rasping breath and tried to sit up straighter. 'I suspect my time has come. I've done my three score and ten.' He paused as another agonising spasm wracked his body. 'All of life has to end sometime,' he wheezed. 'I just wish it would get on with it and be over soon.'

'I don't like to hear you talk like that.' I rearranged the blanket around his shoulders. 'I've got some broth on the stove. That will cheer you up a bit.'

I put some more wood on the fire and lit the candle as late afternoon darkness descended, before bustling off to the kitchen.

Abraham closed his eyes but sleep wouldn't come. His mind wandered back over his life. 'All in all, I've had a good life. There've been struggles surely, but so much fun and satisfaction from my maps. I consider that I may have made a small contribution to this world. And certainly, I'm at peace with my maker.'

As he drifted off, I could see the sunflowers blooming in the garden outside his window and hear the sparrow chicks chirping in the bushes. The wings of a wayward dragonfly bumped into the window. An owl hooted in the distance. I wondered whether Abe was aware of them too.

It was good that nature was his companion as he left this world. I brushed the tears from my eyes.

Epilogue

We asked Justus Lipsius to write the epitaph for Abraham's tomb. What could he say about the man? How could he limit himself to just a few words?

Lipsius finally settled for a piece of which the crux was *Quietis cultor sine lite, uxore, prole*, which roughly translates as 'An inconspicuous worshipper, non-belligerent, celibate, childless' or perhaps 'A tranquil inhabitant with no quarrel, no wife, no offspring'. For Abraham remained above the petty squabbles which so often disturbed the learned and, for the most part, above the political unrest that constantly simmered below the surface of our lives and often broke out in devastating ways. And no doubt it was because he had no wife nor children of his own that he was free to travel all over the world, to meet scholars and find out the latest at first hand, to get the most up-to-date information about all things cartographic and numismatic, and to obtain all the books from which he never stopped learning.

Abraham's own motto in many ways also summed up who he was: *Contemno et orno, mente, manu*, 'I see, I scorn, with my mind and my hand', or more broadly, 'I pay no heed to the world and yet I honour it with my mind and with my hand.'

The city of Antwerp struck a coin in his memory, the expert on coins of antiquity. It was of gold, silver and bronze concentric circles with his portrait on it and the text in Latin, 'Abraham Ortelius of Antwerp', surrounding it. The reverse side had an image of a snake encircling books, a symbol of his attainment of wisdom through the study of books, with the Greek text, 'The foolishness of God', surrounding it. This quote from the letter of Paul to the Corinthians in the Bible reads in full, 'The foolishness of God is wiser than human wisdom, and the weakness of God is stronger than human strength.' That was Abraham, always giving God the glory.

Even in his own lifetime, Abraham had been honoured by the king and by the city of Antwerp. His contemporaries toasted him as the 'Ptolemy of this century'. And yet, amidst it all, he had remained humble and modest.

*

We buried him in St Michael's Abbey. There were outpourings of grief all over Antwerp and probably in many other places in the world at the news of his death.

Although Francis Sweertius, a merchant and an antiquarian, was considerably younger than Abraham, he was a good friend. We first met Sweertius through the humanist group which Abraham led. And they shared an interest in ancient things. Sweertius liked nothing better than to browse in Abraham's museum, browse among the books and antiquities that he had collected.

Sweertius was devastated when Ortelius died. He gathered a collection of eulogies for him called *Lachrymae, Tears of grief.* He also wrote a biographical sketch of Ortelius's life that was included with the eulogies.

He wrote down how he saw the man.

In company he behaved modestly, courteously and had a pleasant and merry posture. Such was his singular humaneness that it wasn't surprising to see how easily he won and retained the love of whoever he met. As far as his enemies were concerned, he preferred to meet them with kindness or ignore them rather than to act in revenge because of their malice. He so much hated vice that he preferred to appreciate virtue even in enemies and strangers. Arguments about divinity or religious disputes he detested and abhorred as being dangerous and pernicious. He preferred deep insight and sound judgement above flattering eloquence or quaint terminology. If dangers or adversities came his way, he endured them with patience rather than with any show of fear. Events that were bitter he endured more successfully than those that were uncertain and hard to assess. During his entire life, he was as unselfish as any man could be. He never set his mind on the riches of this world, always keeping in mind his motto 'I scorn and adorn with mind and hand.' Surely this man had some heavenly guidance, which withdrew him so completely from everyday worries that the most upsetting thing that could happen to him was to be interrupted from studying his books, which he preferred above everything else in this world.

*

When Abraham died in that summer of 1598, he left all of his real estate and funds to me, all his maps, books and collections to his beloved nephew Jacob Colius and his personal papers along with his *album amicorum* to his cousin Emanuel. Jacob wasn't able to come to Antwerp for his funeral or when the will was read. His strong Protestant views made it imprudent for him to do so. Abraham had hoped that Jacob would take up the family antiques and maps business which was still in operation.

Our sister and Emanuel's cousin, Elisabeth Colius, had passed away in London a few years before Abraham left this world.

Even after Abraham died, Plantin's son-in-law, Johannes Moretus, kept on printing copies of the *Theatrum*. From its original seventy maps and eighty-seven bibliographic references in the first edition of 1570, the mapbook would grow through its thirty-one editions to encompass 167 maps and 183 references in 1612. During this period, 7,300 copies were to be printed in seven different languages. A remarkable feat for one man.

Acknowledgements

I have always been fascinated by the historical development of maps that accompanied and gave impetus to the gradual discovery of the world. In fact, I've always appreciated maps of any kind.

Over such a long incubation period, many people have read and critiqued this book. Some told me *where* it needed improving, a few told me *how* to improve it. Grateful thanks to Ray Tyndale, who mentored me through the whole process; to Patrick Allington and Mary Cunnane for their comments on the initial overall structure; to Nicki Hunt, Ian Coulls and Beth Peters, who made many helpful suggestions; to Maureen Mitson and Celia Bolton, who read early drafts; and to Margaret Rawlinson, who looked after me at Wallaroo on a couple of occasions to get the damn thing finished. And especially to Stephen and Brenda Matthews of Ginninderra Press, who kindly published it for me. And lastly, to long-suffering family and friends, who listened countless times to my ravings.

Long and pleasant hours of research went into this book, including a very fruitful trip to Antwerp, where one of Ortelius's houses is still extant but now privately owned, and one to the National Library in Canberra, which hosted a cartographic exhibition, Mapping Our World, in 2013, as well as containing many useful books. The website Cartographica Neerlandica contains invaluable images of each of Ortelius's maps along with their accompanying text.

The State Library of South Australia contains an original *Theatrum Orbis Terrarum* and one of the later editions – indeed things of beauty.

www.ingramcontent.com/pod-product-compliance
Lightning Source LLC
Chambersburg PA
CBHW020332110726
47898CB00003B/844